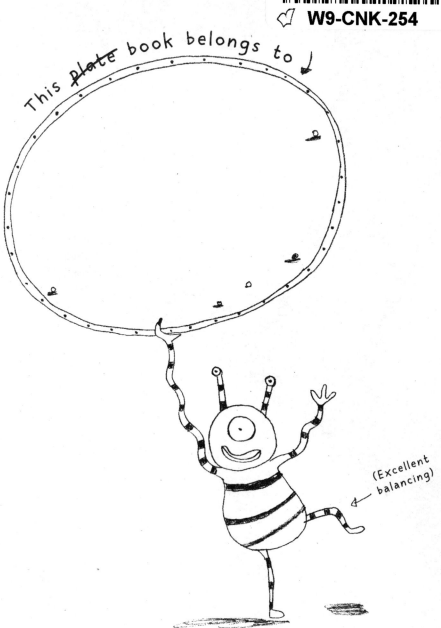

This ~~plate~~ book belongs to

(Excellent balancing)

GENIUS IDEAS (mostly)

Liz Pichon

Wafer balancing (new sport)

SCHOLASTIC

Scholastic Children's Books
An imprint of Scholastic Ltd
Euston House, 24 Eversholt Street
London, NW1 1DB, UK

Registered office: Westfield Road, Southam,
Warwickshire, CV47 0RA
SCHOLASTIC and associated logos are trademarks and/or
registered trademarks of Scholastic Inc.

ISBN 978-93-5103-302-8

Reprinted by Scholastic India Pvt. Ltd., 2014 (Four times),
2015 (Four times), 2016 (Four times), 2017 (Four times)

Printed and bound by MicroPrints (India), New Delhi

www.scholastic.co.uk/zone

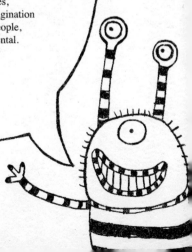

To my sister Lyn ♡ xx

Who made me EXCELLENT toys, bought lovely books and showed me how to draw with fancy pens and crayons.

↗ Fancy crayons

Beddy Byes

(This card was a bit annoying, though)

THIS is a GENIUS idea...

A FLIP BOOK in a book. Watch the bug dance

If my writing looks a bit "WOBBLY", it's because I've just had a

TERRIBLE SHOCK!

So to help me calm "↓" down,

I'm searching 👀 for the

SPECIAL

EMERGENCY BISCUITS

I keep hidden under my bed.

(This is definitely an emergency.)

biscuit crumbs

PHEW! That's better.

OK, let me explain what happened. I was in the bathroom, pretending to have a shower while reading my comic (like you do).

When SOMEONE started KNOCKING really loudly on the door.
I assumed it was my sister Delia ...
... so I ignored her.

Then she did it again ...

... and again ...

... and again.

Knock

Knock

Knock

Knock

The **noise** was very annoying. But I managed to carry on reading ⊙ ⊙ EVERY single page of my comic REALLY slowly. EVENTUALLY when I'd finished, I very CAREFULLY opened the bathroom door. →

I was expecting Delia to SHOUT at me for taking so long. I wasn't expecting to see this. →

It was a HORRIBLE Sight! I let out a LOUD

ARGH!

Which made Dad come running out of the bedroom to see what all the **noise** was about. He said, "What's the problem here?" So I said, "Delia's the problem. She **looks SCARY** without her  ← sunglasses!"

Then Dad said it would be **nice** to have just ONE morning without being (disturbed) by the two of us ♪**ARGUING.**

Delia got REALLY CROSS and pointed at ME,  saying I was the only one who was "DISTURBED". Then she told Dad that he looked

totally ridiculous.

Before disappearing into the bathroom and

slamming the door.

Which left me in

FULL VIEW

of what Dad was wearing.

BRIGHT blue cycling shorts.

I was speechless.

I couldn't decide who looked WORSE:

Delia without her sunglasses or Dad in his cycling shorts ∏ ? Mum wasn't much help either. She came upstairs and

SHOUTED, "Why is everyone shouting?"

Followed quickly by "And what on EARTH are you wearing?" Dad pointed out that she was the only one who was shouting and the ∏ cycling shorts were all part of his

Carefully planned new fitness regime.

Which made Mum LAUGH out loud. ha! ha! ha!

I decided that this was probably a good time to head back to my room because:

NASTY SURPRISES + SHOCKS =
→ EMERGENCY BISCUITS

It's a good job I keep a few hidden for these kinds of situations. I just hope there are no more unwanted surprises today. Sigh... I eat half of the (second) emergency wafer and start to imagine what MY idea of a FUN AND VERY RELAXING day at school would be. Mmmmmmm ... I think it would probably go something like this...

 **M**r Fullerman is **DELIGHTED** to see me (even though I'm late).

 Hello, Tom, **VERY** good to see you.

I have my own special **COMFY** chair and table that are as → far away as possible from that very annoying **M**arcus **M**eldrew.

sneaky snack box

far away

Marcus

comfy chair

L essons are OPTIONAL so I can choose what I want to do (which is easy).

Choose Your
LESSONS Today

ART	✗
MATHS	✓
Doodling	✓
MUSIC	✗
Spelling	
FUN Experiments	✓

Our NICE new art teacher Miss Straw insists I do a WHOLE art project on ...

CARAMEL WAFERS.

Really? If you insist   I have *f u n* arranging them into towers before spending as MUCH time as I want drawing and doodling.

Sigh

Miss Straw is VERY impressed   Well done, Tom!   and lets me eat TWO wafers for my snack.

AND I'm allowed to unwrap the others and use the foil for my interesting wafer collage.

(The wafers I can save to eat later.)

Miss Straw thinks I am an ART BISCUIT GeNiuS.

I agree.

Well done, Tom.

What can I say? You deserve 100 merits for this AMAZING collage!

Miss Straw,

(I show my 100 merits to Marcus, which annoys him.)

Then the day gets even better. A few friends and I have a DELICIOUS lunch served by ...

... the teachers.

More iced water, Tom?

I eat in the best part of the dinner hall (for a change). I'm allowed to have SECONDS of pudding, followed by a relaxing rest with my feet up before the next lesson starts.

Which is

EXTRA FUN EXPERIMENTS.

(Outside - because it would be SUNNY on my perfect day.)

The whole class helps me place hundreds of WAFERS in a **l o n g** row around the school. Then I get to *PUSH* the first wafer forward, causing them all to fall one by one in an

AMAZING pattern (like dominoes).

Solid

Amy Porter

The SPECTACULAR WAFER DISPLAY

breaks the WORLD BISCUIT FALLING RECORD!

YEAH!

(And everyone gets to eat a few more of them too.)

Then as a **special** treat, **M**r Fullerman announces that our **MUSIC LESSON** today will be taught by ... **DUDE 3**, only the **BEST BAND** EVER! Who arrive at our school in their fancy ↕ **HUGE** tour bus. They put on a fantastic concert for the entire school, and because Derek (my best mate) and I are **DUDE 3** 's **BIGGEST** fans, we get to stand on stage and play along with our own guitars to all the songs that we know. **DUDE 3** congratulate **US** on how good **WE** are. Which makes **M**arcus pull a face like this: Huh?

But that's NOTHING ...

compared to the LOOK on Delia's face

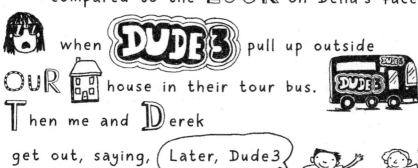 when DUDE3 pull up outside

OUR house in their tour bus.

Then me and Derek

get out, saying, (Later, Dude3)

to the whole band,

who wave back.

Then we carry our BRAND

NEW COOL guitars that the band have

given us back to the house.

Now THAT'S MY idea of the BEST and MOST AMAZING DAY at school EVER!

Oh well... You never know. Today might turn out to be a **GOOD** day after all? Like **LAST WEEK** in assembly (which I wasn't looking forward to), **M**rs **N**ap ➡️ asked everyone a question.

> Who can tell me what month it is and what year?

Before I could put **UP** my hand to answer, **M**arcus **M**eldrew practically **LEAPT** off the floor, waving his arm around, so **M**rs **N**ap would pick him. She did.

But the REALLY funny bit was when **M**rs **N**ap asked Marcus to sit down and he accidentally said **LOUDLY**,

> **Y**es, **M**umm**y**.

Then he couldn't understand why we were all LAUGHING  so much. Mrs Nap had to say,

> I think you meant to say
> YES, Mrs Nap.

It was HILARIOUS! I laughed a LOT that day. Right NOW, though, if Mum and Dad see how late I am, I'll be in trouble. Although I'm not sure they'd notice. I can still hear Mum chuckling EVERY time she says the words fitness regime like it's the FUNNIEST joke she's EVER heard.

I'm not laughing because I know that:

DAD + FITNESS REGIME = LOADS MORE DODGY SPORTS OUTFITS FIT

There's a good chance that he could start turning up at my school, or WORSE STILL, my friends' houses, wearing something EVEN more embarrassing than those BRIGHT BLUE CYCLING SHORTS.

IF THAT'S POSSIBLE?

I slip downstairs and grab some breakfast and realize that I am <u>properly</u> late for school now. **M**um is upstairs and still a bit busy.

I could go and ask her to write me a nice LATE NOTE to give to

(Mum being busy)

ha! ha!

Mr **F**ullerman, which would probably stop me from getting into any trouble? OK, TOM

But why bother when it's **SO** much easier ...

... just to write one myself.

(A genius idea.)

Dear Mr Fullerman,

Poor Tom has had a VERY nasty shock this morning due to his ~~rotten stupid~~ sister scaring him. I'm very sorry he's late for school. His sister has been warned not to scare him again (or else).

Because of his SHOCK, Tom might find it hard to concentrate on any tricky maths today. Just letting you know.

Thank you,

Rita Gates

There, all done!
(Hopefully Mr Fullerman won't suspect anything dodgy about my note. I didn't mention Dad's shorts, as that would take too long to explain.)

Dad comes downstairs and starts doing some weird kinds of stretching moves.

Mum is SHOUTING from upstairs to me:

Have you gone yet, Tom?

So I say BYE to Dad quickly and remind him I might be going to Norman's house for a band practice tonight. He says, "Norman's house isn't too far. How about I run over and collect you?" And I say,

"NO WAY!"

just that little bit too quickly in case he

decides to turn up looking like ...

well, like that. ➡

I tell him Derek's dad is coming to pick us up.

"All sorted, no need to worry, Dad."

Good thinking ...

phew!

D erek's not waiting outside: he's already left for school. So I set off  with my **SPECIAL** LATE NOTE safely in my bag.

As I walk past the shop, I'm (thinking) maybe I could **POP** in for a small snack? (Good idea.) It takes me a while to choose what to have.

mmmmm?

FRUIT CHews

But because I have a LATE NOTE, I'm hoping Mr Fullerman will read it and say, **That's all fine, Tom** then let me off the hook.

And if he doesn't, at least I'll have my snack to eat.

Fingers crossed.

When I finally arrive at school, no one is around. It's REALLY quiet EVERYWHERE. Apart from Mrs Nap's classroom, where I can hear some odd noises WAFTING out of her slightly open door.

It sounds a bit like ...

CATS YOWLING IN PAIN.

Owww {w} w'w

Awwwww

I go and take a sneaky 👁 👁 peek to see what's going on.

It is Mrs Nap.

She seems to be Singing the WHOLE register?

Worse than that, Mrs Nap is making the class sing their names back to her. One by one. Which is PAINFUL to hear.

Charlie Smith?

Charlie Smith is here, Mrs Nap

Mrs Nap is being her usual cheerful self when she sings.

"Isn't this FUN, everyone?"

And Charlie Smith (who's just sung his name) sings back, "NOOOOO, not really."

Which makes Mrs Nap a bit CROSS. So she sings, "Oh dear ... let's sing it again from the beginning and this time we'll ALL do it properly."

Charlie Smith tries to sing, "I was only joking, Mrs Nap!" But it's too late.

Luckily for me (and my class) Mr Fullerman doesn't do "register singing". I think we'd be there ALL day if he did.

I'm SO busy peering in the classroom that I don't hear Mrs Mumble behind me until she says,

> Hello, Tom.

Which makes me JUMP.

"Shouldn't you be in class?"

I explain I was on the way there and I have a LATE NOTE.  Mrs Mumble remembers there's a "special buddy talk this morning. Mr Fullerman was taking your class to meet some of the younger children."

So I say, "Great."

And I'm about to go off and find them.

T hen she adds,  "But I'm not sure WHICH class they've gone to. Best you wait in the school office with ⌐me⌐ until they're back so I can mark ✓ you in the register. We don't want you just wandering round school, do we?"

(Me wandering)

I'm (thinking...)

1. What **I͟S** a "buddy talk"?
2. How long will I have to sit in the school office for, as it can be a *BIT* awkward?

What are you doing here, Tom

Mrs Mumble points to a seat and asks me
not to talk while she makes an announcement
over the **loudspeaker.**
At least this should be
fun to watch.

Mrs Mumble clears her throat
and _LEANS_ into the speaker
while pushing a special RED button.
As soon as she starts speaking, her voice
goes all, well ...

Mumbly.

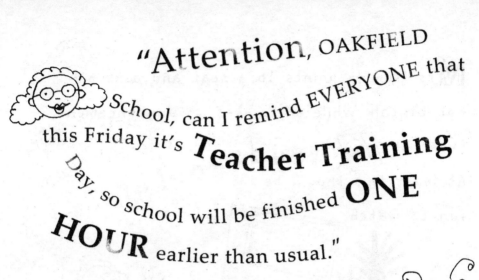

"Attention, OAKFIELD School, can I remind EVERYONE that this Friday it's Teacher Training Day, so school will be finished ONE HOUR earlier than usual."

I can just about hear *CHeers* coming from all over the school (which is funny).

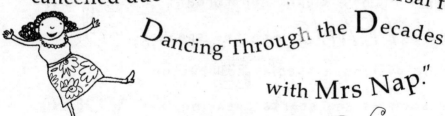

"This lunchtime's chess club is cancelled due to an EXTRA rehearsal for Dancing Through the Decades with Mrs Nap."

Another slightly smaller *CHeer* goes around.

The finishes by telling everyone...

"One more thing. When Mr Fullerman returns to his class, could he send someone to collect **TOM GATES** from the school office, as he was **LATE** for school and is waiting in the office to be **COLLECTED**. Thank you."

huh?

GREAT, now the **WHOLE** school knows I'm late. **AND** Mrs Mumble has made me sound like I'm some kind of **PARCEL**.

(Groan.)

TOM GATES
(For collection)
THIS WAY UP

As Mrs Mumble's finished her message, I MUST remind her about my LATE NOTE so I don't get into trouble.

I say, "Mrs Mumble, I know I'm LATE but I have a NOTE to explain why."

And she says, "That's good, Tom. I'd like to SEE that note."

Which makes me PANIC a bit.

My note is stuffed into my bag and I can't find it anywhere.

I put my bag down on to her desk so I can have a good rummage around. While I'm looking, I carefully explain ALL about my OLDER sister  Delia and how she gave me a NASTY SHOCK this morning (which is true, she did). But I don't say what happened. Instead I recreate my "I'M SHOCKED!" face like this...

Which startles Mrs Mumble a bit.

And because I STILL can't find my note, I carry on...

"It's in here somewhere."
Then I tell Mrs Mumble how Mum
was a bit worried about me
because I looked slightly PALE.

"Mum told me I was CLAMMY
from the SHOCK and I needed to sit down
and recover a bit before going to school.
Which is why I'm late, Mrs Mumble."
I do a slightly different type of face ... like
this...

Then breathe a SIGH of relief,
as I've just found my note. I give it to Mrs
Mumble, who's about to read
it when there's a
KNOCK at the office door.

It's **AMY PORTER** from my class. She tells **Mrs Mumble** TWO things.

1. I can come back to class, as **Mr Fullerman** is there now.

I'm back

2. The **WHOLE** school have just heard my why I'm LATE explanation because the

LOUDSPEAKER is still on.

IT IS?

Mrs Mumble LIFTS my bag off the SPECIAL red button and says,

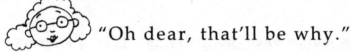 "Oh dear, that'll be why."

I'm doing a "VERY embarrassed" face, which looks like this...

Shame

Groan.

And if that's not bad enough, Mrs Mumble

only goes and brings out her

She says, "That reminds

me, Tom – I need a picture of you."

I say, "RIGHT NOW?"

Because I can feel my face going even

REDDER!

Mrs Mumble tells me that it's for the

school NEWSLETTER.

"You have a

SPECIAL MENTION

for the EXCELLENT DRAWING HOMEWORK*

on your school book. Nothing to be

embarrassed about, Tom!"

*See page 357, Everything's Amazing (Sort Of).

Which **cheers** me up a bit. **I**'d forgotten about being in the NEWSLETTER.

At least **AMY** will see that I don't make stupid mistakes like this *all* the time. Speaking of stupid mistakes...

Mrs **M**umble is just about to take the photo when someone else **knocks** at the door. There's a kid

standing outside with a COMB ... ... STUCK in his hair.

Mrs Mumble looks at him and says, "How did you do that?"

The kid says he's not really sure.

Mrs Mumble tells him to Wait there, then goes ahead and takes what I hope will be a VERY Nice picture of me for the NEWSLETTER.

SMILE

Now Mrs Mumble's got this kid with a comb stuck in his hair to deal with, my seems to have *Slipped* her notice, which is a

BIG RELIEF. ~Phew

On the way back to class, **AMY PORTER** wants to know exactly what Delia did that gave me such a **SHOCK**. I *can't* say "She took off her sunglasses, it was terrible" because **that** doesn't sound shocking at all. (Even though it was.)

Instead I say, "It was nothing, I'm over it now." (Like I'm being brave.)

Then I manage to quickly change the subject by asking **AMY** what the **BUDDY TALK** was all about. **AMY** says the **YOUNGER** kids get to choose an older kid (one of us) to be their **BUDDY.**

"We have to look out for them and make sure they're happy in school. That kind of thing. Mr Fullerman took us to say hello so the little kids know who we all are now." I say, "Lucky them."

My class

Pick me!

Since I wasn't there, I ask **AMY** what happens if you don't get chosen to be a buddy. **AMY** tells me,

"Not <u>all</u> the little kids want to have buddies. So don't worry, it will be less hassle for you not to be picked."

But I think I'd make a good **BUDDY**. I could show them all kinds of really **important** stuff, like:

○ **How** to be **first** in the lunch queue.

sneaky short cuts

Oh yes!

- **H**ow to get **BIG** portions of the food you like.

- **H**ow to get small portions of the food you don't like.

- **W**hich teachers to look👀 out for.

Mrs Worthing**TASH**ton

Mr Fullerman

Mr Keen

Mr Sprocket

Mrs Nap

Don't mention her ... moustache.

Beady eyes

BEWARE school concerts

Avoid her singing

- **W**hy **DUDE3** are the **BEST BAND** in the whole world ...

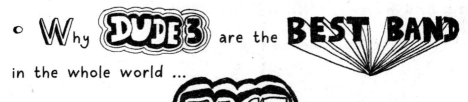

FACT

Back in class, **Mr Fullerman** says,

Better late than NEVER, Tom.

I don't have to explain where I've been

because everyone has already heard.

(Groan.)

Marcus Meldrew can't WAIT to tell

me how STUPID I sounded over the

loudspeaker.

You sounded stupid

So I tell him,

"You don't need a LOUDSPEAKER

to SOUND STUPID."

And he says, "No one will pick you as a buddy

because you weren't there."

So I (think) quickly and say,
"No one will pick YOU as a buddy
because you [WERE] there."

Then Mr Fullerman GLARES at
both of us and says,

 **STOP TALKING.**

Which shuts Marcus up ... for now.

Mr Fullerman says today he's going to
read us a story. (I'm hoping this means
we'll have a nice RELAXing

day after all?)

T hen he adds...

"**Listen** carefully, as we'll be doing some work about the story later."

(Groan...)

M r F ullerman holds up a book and asks if anyone has heard of

Aesop's Fables?

And Mark Clump, who hardly EVER puts his hand up, gets VERY EXCITED and says,

Mr Fullerman, I HAVE, I HAVE. They're my favourite.

Mr Fullerman asks Mark,

Which is your FAVOURITE FABLE, Mark?

And Mark Clump thinks for a while...

(Quite a long while, actually.)

Mr Fullerman looks impressed that Mark is thinking about his answer SO carefully.

Until he says...

Plain if it's toasted with butter

and jam ... yum.

Which isn't quite the answer
Mr Fullerman was expecting.

The class start LAUGHING Ha! Ha! Ha! Ha! Ha!
because we've just realized Mark thinks
Mr Fullerman said BAGEL.

Whoops

So just to make it clear for everyone,

M r Fullerman says,

The FABLE –
[NOT] BAGEL, FABLE –
I'll be reading is called
"THE BOY WHO CRIED WOLF".

Marcus nudges me and says he knows this

story already.

The wolf eats the boy in the
end ... that's it, really.

Thanks for telling me the

ending, Marcus.

That's just great.

The good news is Marcus has given me 😊 an idea 💡 for a doodle. I carefully arrange a few innocent-looking books on my desk.

While Mr Fullerman is reading out the story, I get busy drawing.

AMY is watching 👧 and smiling. I have to keep stopping to pay attention to

Mr Fullerman.

(Me paying attention.)

Marcus has been ignoring me. Until right at the end of my drawing, when I do a 😠 picture of him ...

... that catches his eye.

Marcus has only gone and put his hand UP and interrupted Mr Fullerman, who's not very happy.

He tells Mr Fullerman,

"Sir! Tom Gates is drawing, SIR."

Luckily for me, Mr Fullerman doesn't tell me off. I just have to put down my pen and LISTEN.

Which I do (for a while).

 **B**ut **M**arcus is **still** watching me.

Which is annoying.

So I start to draw this line

Hey!

| Marcus ⟹ Yes, **YOU.** Follow this line

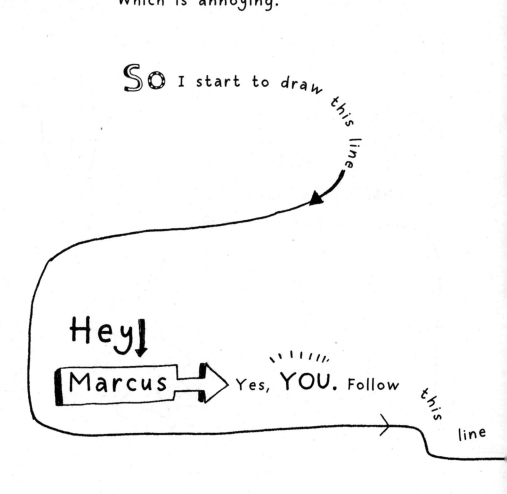

Don't stop looking!

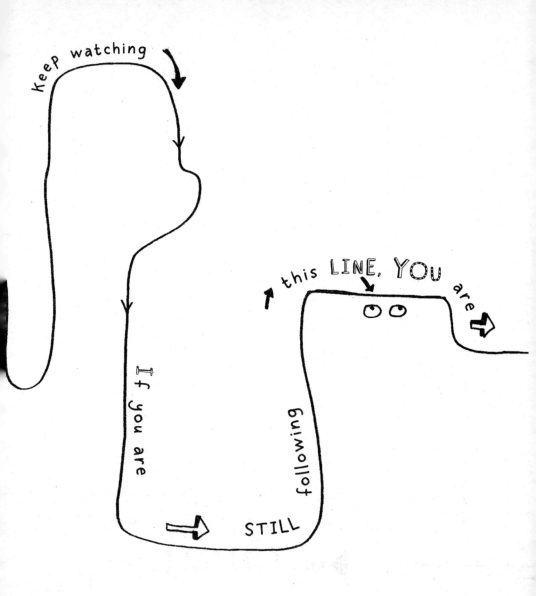

Keep watching

this LINE, YOU are

I f you are

following

If you are

STILL

AN IDIOT!

Ha!
Ha!
Ha!
Ha!
Ha!

Marcus looks like this now.

(I should try this trick

on Delia too!)

Break-Time
(at LAST)

My best mate Derek ⟹ 😊 comes to find me. He can't come to band 🎸 practice tonight, which is a shame.

😕 "I have to go to Aunt Julia's house with my mum." Derek looks really fed up.
"I hope she doesn't do that face-**Squeeze** thing on me again.
It's embarrassing."

> Look at you!

← Aunt Julia

To make Derek feel better, I tell him about when my **A**unty Alice, 🤓 **U**ncle Kevin 😊 and the cousins 😊 😊 came round for a family barbecue last weekend.

Derek says, "I **LOVE** barbecues."
And I say, "So do I, usually."

I explain to Derek,

"It would have been OK, but Dad

was in a REALLY BAD mood, mostly

because of Uncle Kevin and his dodgy jokes.

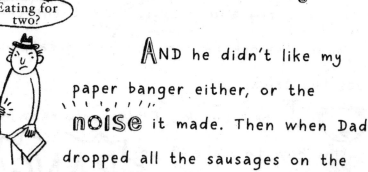

Eating for two?

AND he didn't like my

paper banger either, or the

noise it made. Then when Dad

dropped all the sausages on the

ground, he said it was MY fault!"

Derek says, "I was wondering where Rooster got those sausages from. And what's a paper banger*?"

I still have a paper banger **Scrunched** up in my pocket. So I take it out and try and smooth out the creases to make it work better. It's not great, but it does the trick.

I tell Derek, "I was only showing the cousins how to make it go **BANG!**

Like this ... by flicking it over my head..." **BANG**

*See page 308 on how to make a paper banger.

Derek seems to have cheered up  a bit and wants to have a go at making the paper banger work himself.

It takes a few tries,

duff

but eventually Derek gets it at the right angle

Bang!

... to make a very loud

BANG!

The noise attracts a bit of attention from some of the little kids in school, who come over and want to know

What's that?

"It's a paper banger," I tell them. "Look."
Then I show them how it works.
"You can make them yourself,
it's easy."

BANG!

This kid called **Joey** wants to take a closer look.  **H**e's the one I saw in the school office with the comb stuck in his hair (which is out now).

I'm very nice and let **Joey** have a go. I show him the knack of making the banger work properly too. **W**hich is a mistake...

He manages to TEAR ALL the paper up the sides. Joey says sorry and hands it back to me. It's just as well they're easy to make, because this one's ruined.

Derek says **Joey** reminds him of **N**orman when he breaks stuff. **M**ind you, ever since **N**orman fell off his bike* and hurt his  elbows, he's been a bit more careful about everything he does.

> Mind that banana skin

Derek reminds me to tell Norman that we'll have to cancel band practice tonight. He suggests, "We could do it at the weekend instead?" **A**nd then he says **AGAIN**, "You won't forget to tell Norman, will you, Tom?" And I say,

> As if!

* See page 247 of Everything's Amazing (Sort Of) for the full story.

PE

(Stands for **P**hysical **E**ducation, or in **N**orman's case, **P**oorly **E**lbows.)

Even though **N**orman is the FIRST person I see when I come into class, I completely forget to tell him about band practice. **N**orman gets to miss PE because of his elbows.

I ask him if he's being allowed to **relax** for a bit or do something else? **N**orman points to some worksheets and tells me, "**M**r **F**ullerman wants me to catch up with these. He says the class have done them already."

We have?

I take a quick look, but I don't remember doing **ANY** of these worksheets? I'll keep quiet and won't mention it in case **Mr Fullerman** wants me to catch up as well.

Tom!

Norman has to go and sit in the **school office** with **Mrs Mumble** (Ready, Norman?) (Groan.) (like I did), while the rest of class **5F** follow **Mr Fullerman** for **PE**.

Follow me!

We get changed and go outside to the playing fields, as the weather is nice and WARM.

Mr Fullerman announces to the class that we're about to have

LOTS of FUN!

And we all cheer!

"YEAHHH!"

Then he adds,

Training for our SPORTS DAY!

Which makes us go...

"Awwwwwwwwwwww."

 Training doesn't sound like much fun to me?

Mr Fullerman tells us to

by running round the field ➡

Solid (who's not keen on running)
puts up his hand and says,
"Mr Fullerman, I am really
WARM already, so do I
have to run?"

I think Solid has made a
VERY good point.

So I say, 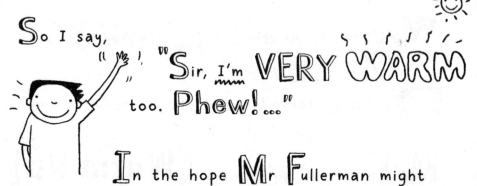 "Sir, I'm VERY WARM too. Phew!..."

In the hope Mr Fullerman might change his mind about making us do all that running.

NO chance.

Mr Fullerman says,

TWICE round the playing fields for EVERYONE.

Ignoring both of us.

The whole class are GROANING now and 👀 👀 👀 👀 👀 staring at us. Apart from Brad Galloway, who loves running. Yes!

Florence Mitchell's not happy.

She says,

Nice work, Tom.

Whoops...

Like it's ALL MY FAULT!

Mr Fullerman is keeping his BEADY EYES on ME the WHOLE time I'm running. I can't even hide behind a TREE or pretend to be doing up my shoelaces for a quick REST without him shouting,

"Keep going, TOM ... I can SEE YOU!"

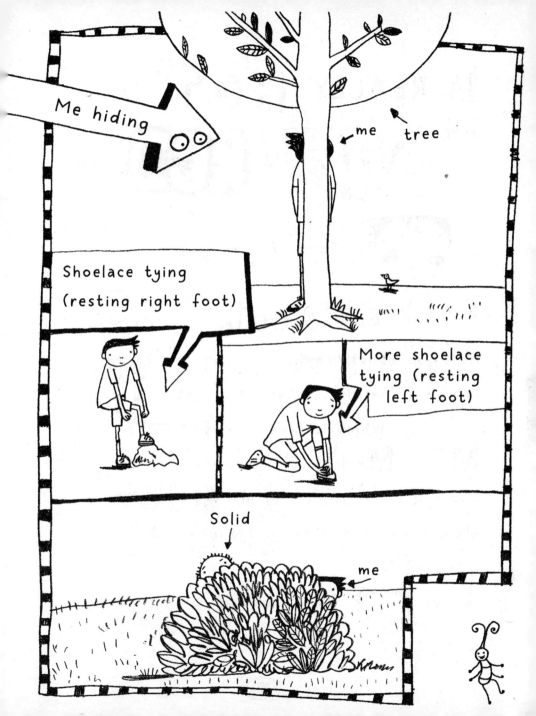

I'm REALLY HOT and I've gone BRIGHT RED now.

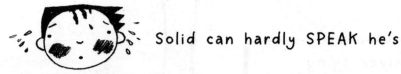 Solid can hardly SPEAK he's

SO PUFFED out.

He (just about) says,

"We ... hardly ... started ... yet."

Which is true. (Groan.)

Marcus Meldrew comes over to ME

and starts WaviNg his hands

around my head. (Which is annoying.)

I say, "What are you doing, Marcus?"

And he says,

"**M**y hands are **COLD**, I'm just warming them up ...

ON YOUR FACE!"

Ha! Ha! **HA! HA!**

Marcus thinks he's **HILARIOUS.**

I think it's going to be a VERY **long PE** lesson.

Groan.

My class, 5F, have **never** (I repeat) **NEVER** won **ANYTHING** on SPORTS DAY. We're a bit rubbish compared to some of the other classes.

Every year at the end of SPORTS DAY Mr Fullerman says,

"WELL DONE, Class 5F, you've ALL done SO WELL! Just remember, it's the taking part that counts."

(Even though we've come last.)

While Mr Sprocket's class, Class 5S, are usually

✶ ★ Celebrating ⁂ ...

by **WHOOPING** and **CHEERING**

because they have won

SPORTS DAY

AGAIN.

SPORTS DAY

Go Class 5S!

(Mr Sprocket doing his VICTORY

ROBOT DANCE.)

Right now, from the way Mr Fullerman is making us do STAR  JUMPS

and bunny hops

(which are hurting my legs),

I think he's hoping that

THIS time SPORTS DAY

could be a bit different for

EVERYONE.

At LAST!

SPORTS DAY

Sometimes I wonder why SPORTS DAY is actually called SPORTS DAY. I'm not sure EVERYTHING we do is a REAL sport?

Like...

Hula Hooping

Which is a LOT harder than it looks.

Skipping

Mr Fullerman says boxers skip to keep fit. But they probably don't have someone like Marcus standing RIGHT NEXT to them messing up THEIR skipping ROPE all the time.

Beanbag juggling

BEANBAGS get used a LOT on SPORTS DAY:

we do loads of throwing and catching

and running in between them.

My personal favourite is beanbag balancing. It's fun to put them on your arms, knees, or do a double balance on your knee and foot at the same time. I often pile them on my head. Mr Fullerman tells me to stop when I get to about here.

The LONG jump is the only "sport" we do today that I've seen 👁 👁 on telly.

Mr Fullerman wants all of us to have a go.

He tells us,

"You need a good *run* up, then throw ⟿ your 🦵🦵 legs forward and jump into the sandpit."

Marcus starts bending his legs up and down. I say, "What are you doing, Marcus?" and he says, "I'm getting ready to do a VERY BIG jump, because I am really good at long jump." Now he's taking deep breaths as well (which is a bit odd).

Solid says to me, "Maybe he is good at long jump after all?"

I say, "Let's see."

We watch Marcus as he starts to **RUN** as fast as he possibly can towards the sandpit...

Then he LEAPS into the air and does a really really ...

... small   jump.

OOOOFFFFF

Mr Fullerman says,

> **Good try, Marcus. Stretch your legs out next time.**

Now Marcus thinks he's done a BRILLIANT jump.

(He hasn't.)

Mr Fullerman finishes off our training session with what he says is a **WARM** DOWN.

Solid says the warm down is making him even **HOTTER.**

On the way back to school, I can hear Marcus telling ANYONE who'll listen that <u>he is</u> a natural at long jump. (He's not.)

Brad Galloway is doing that funny thing when you walk behind someone really closely and they don't know you're there. He's right behind Solid, copying everything he does. Solid doesn't notice for ages, until I tell him. He says, Good joke, Brad and wants to try it on someone else now.

Trouble is, Solid's a bit **TALL** and **noisy** and his shadow keeps giving him away.

I know you're there, Solid

Hello, Solid

When we get back to school, Mr Fullerman asks us to help put away the "sports equipment" (I think he means the beanbags, hula hoops and skipping ropes).

Then he takes the opportunity to remind us how little time there is before SPORTS DAY.

Like we didn't already know.
He says,

Team 5F, you are all going to do AMAZINGLY well this year, I can tell...

Blah blah blah

But it's hard to concentrate when I can see THIS. PTO

Brad is going crazy behind Mr Fullerman's back.

I'm trying not to laugh, but it's almost impossible! Everyone who can see Brad dancing starts laughing too.

Mr Fullerman gets a bit cross and says,

"This is NO laughing matter, Class 5F!"

Ha! Ha!

Ha!

Ha!

Ha!

Ha!

Ha!

Ha!

Ha!

Ha!

Because he can sense something is going on behind his back. Then **M**r **F**ullerman spins round SUPER FAST, just in time to catch Brad Galloway ...

97

... doing absolutely **nothing.**

(Lucky escape or what?)

Mr Fullerman says, **"I'll be keeping a close eye on YOU**, Brad."

Which is excellent news for <u>ME</u>, because (in between doing some work) I've been trying to finish my SUPER LARGE doodle in class.

Which is tricky to do with **M**r **F**ullerman STARING at me (like he does).

Tom, stop doodling

Brad, stop dancing

I can't **WAIT** until lunchtime to catch up with Norman and Derek and tell them **ALL** about how **BRAD** was dancing behind **M**r **F**ullerman's back.

In the dinner hall, I stand up to show them EXACTLY what he did. Like this: I am very busy **WAFTING** my arms around over my head and from side to *side*, recreating Brad's dance. I don't even **NOTICE** that DEREK is making a funny face at me. ⇨

I carry on and say, "Trust me ... it was **REALLY** funny! Especially when **M**r **F**ullerman was going **ON** and **ON** about SPORTS DAY

 and Brad Galloway was wobbling

his legs about like this..."

Then I tell them that the BEST

part of all was that

Mr Fullerman had ABSOLUTELY NO idea

what Brad was doing behind his back.

Derek nudges me and says...

"I think he does now."

Because Mr Fullerman is lOOking over in MY direction with his BEADY eyes and shaking his head in a very STERN and disapproving way. I have a horrible feeling that he's heard everything I've just said.

It's easy to forget about Mr Fullerman's SUPERHUMAN HEARING.

I should have known better. (It's happened to me before.)

Stop eating snacks, Tom!

Huh?

Big distance

Norman says, "He's still looking."

I try and focus REALLY hard on my lunch and whisper,

"Tell me when he's stopped."

Then [two] VERY important questions suddenly `POP` into my head.

Question 1. Will Brad get into trouble because of me?

Question 2. Are those REALLY chips on top of my cake?

Answer 1. Mmmmm, possibly?

Answer 2. Yes, they are really chips because Granny Mavis has been cooking again.

I manage to carefully pick out the chips and eat the cake (the two don't usually go together unless you're Granny Mavis 😊). Norman seems keen to eat my chips, which is fine by me (but a bit weird).

Yum

Then while he's eating, I ask Norman what it was like missing PE and having to do his work in the school office. And he says it was all right. But he did find out something interesting. And Derek and I both say, WHAT'S that?

Norman tells us that he overheard a conversation in Mr Keen's office with Mrs Mumble.

He says, "They were both talking about **BANDS**."

"Really?"

Norman carries on, "I was being very quiet and not moving around much so I could listen. I heard Mr Keen say,

Norman NOT moving

"If we can get **DUDE 3** to play for the school, that would be GREAT. The children would enjoy seeing them."

And I say,

"**Are you sure?**" And Norman says with a mouthful of chips,

Yes, I'm sure.

Derek wonders why **DUDE 3** would want to play at OUR school? If it DOES turn out that **DUDE 3** are playing in our school, that would be...

BRILL

AMA

FANTAST

Derek warns me that I shouldn't get TOO

excited

"I mean, Norman's not totally sure Mr Keen said **DUDE3**. He might have got it wrong. No offence, Norman," Derek adds.

"None taken," Norman says.

But it's true. Norman does get stuff muddled up sometimes.

Oh?

I said bring a PEN, Norman.

TOY HEN

We're getting ready to leave the dinner hall
when we hear a MASSIVE

CRASH!

It's a BIG vegetable accident
with a WHOLE tray of PEAS
being spilled all over the floor.

We're trying to see exactly what happened.

Looks like it was that kid Joey (the one who broke my paper banger).

He's accidentally BUMPED into someone who was carrying the peas.

I can hear Caretaker Stan's keys jingling in the distance already, as he dashes to the dinner hall ...

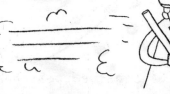

squashed peas

... with a SUPER large BROOM
to get the peas under control.
(Which is proving very difficult to do.)

We leave Stan swishing his broom around with
a LONG trail of squashed peas behind us.

Mr Fullerman asks everyone to **STAND UP** -

THEN **SIT DOWN** -

then **STAND UP** again and check under their shoes for  ←"squashed peas".

(This is another sneaky way of making us practice for SPORTS DAY.)

AMY checks her shoes (which are clean). Marcus has pea-free shoes as well. But mine are COVERED in peas.

Marcus says it looks like I squashed a frog

 and then he makes a big deal of moving

his chair right away from me. Mr Fullerman

hands me a few paper towels, which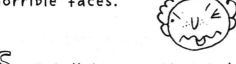

get rid of the peas nicely.

Marcus keeps saying YUCK! and pulling

horrible faces.

So I tell Marcus that he's got something

 GREEN stuck between his

teeth that doesn't look so

good either. He hasn't ,

but it shuts him up for a bit.

Mr Fullerman wants Marcus to

MOVE his chair BACK to where

it was. And stop being so silly.

I agree...

Here's my doodle of Marcus inspired by peas.

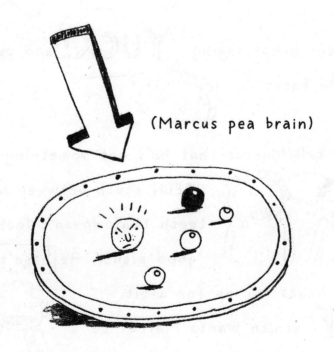

(Marcus pea brain)

ENGLISH

Eventually we get the **S**quashed peas under control, and **M**r **F**ullerman hands out **TWO** WORKSHEETS while making us do some extra arm stretches at the same time.

Stretch up!

He says everyone can choose which worksheet to do. Then he STARES at Brad and says,

"Brad, you might like to do worksheet one? And don't forget, I do have eyes in the back of my head."

Which sounds like an odd thing for **M**r **F**ullerman to say. **STOP pulling faces, Brad**

Until I read worksheet one. (Brad's been

rumbled.)

Creative Writing Project 1

Read the beginning of this story carefully. Then I'd like YOU to continue the story on a separate piece of paper. Please write at least one A4 page.

It was clear to Mr Fullerman that

SOMETHING was going on behind his

back. He decided the only thing to do

was ...

go home.

The end.

If I were going to write an ending for the story on worksheet one, I'd do this... Ha! Ha!

Bit short, I know. Better do worksheet two instead

if I don't want to get into trouble (again).

Creative Writing Project 2

I would like you to write your own fable with a similar theme to the fable we read in class, "The Boy Who Cried Wolf". The story can be from your own imagination or based on something that might have happened to you in your own life.

At least one A4 page, please.

This is my version of a FABLE – all based on the family barbecue I was telling Derek about earlier that we had last weekend. Enjoy.

The Boy Who Said,

The Sausages Are Burnt

By Tom Gates

This is the story of a family who wouldn't listen to their **VERY** smart son ➞ (that will be me, then). It all began when the **SUN** came out and my dad thought it would be an **EXCELLENT** idea to have a barbecue. I said,

Doesn't it always rain when you get out the barbecue, Dad?

And he said,

Don't be daft, of course it's NOT going to rain!

118

(Like *THAT'S* never happened before.)

So I watched Dad wheel the barbecue out
from the corner of the garden.

It was covered with some special protective plastic that Dad told me would keep it

EXTRA clean and ready to use in an instant!

But underneath the "protective plastic" the barbecue was full of revolting **gunge**.

I told Dad the barbecue didn't look THAT clean? And Dad said that it just needed a quick brush down and all that BLACK **gunge** would BURN off during cooking.

I said,

Are you sure? It looks really disgusting.

But Dad wasn't listening to me. He was looking at Mum, who was *RUNNING* towards us in a very **BIG PANIC**.  She told Dad,

I've COMPLETELY forgotten that Uncle Kevin and Aunty Alice and the cousins are coming to lunch...

Dad said, When? And Mum said, TODAY... Which would have been OK until she added... In five minutes! Dad said, "Oh great." (But not in a *JOLLY* way.) Mum wanted to know how long the barbecue would take? And I said, "It will take FOREVER, it always does."

121

But Dad said, Don't listen to Tom.

And gave me a LOOK.

He ASSURED Mum that he knew EXACTLY

what he was doing. "I can just throw on a

couple of extra  sausages for them."

← Extra sausages

(Without wanting to SPOIL the story,

you can probably see what's happening here.)

Dad + NOT listening to me ➡ = DISASTER

When Uncle Kevin arrived EARLY,

Dad was busy telling Mum that EVERYTHING

would be fine because he was a

barbecue expert. ☺

And Uncle Kevin said,

> HELLO! Did someone say barbecue expert? I'm here!

And Dad whispered, "Great, that's all I need." So Mum suggested that we should leave both the barbecue experts to get on with **burning** the lunch.

Which Dad didn't think was very funny.

All this talk of sausages was making me hungry. I really HOPED the barbecue wasn't going to take too long.

Aunty Alice and the cousins were in the kitchen holding a MASSIVE bag of snacks. I told them they should EAT them NOW because the barbecue could take AGES. Aunty Alice looked SURPRISED and said,

You're having a barbecue? I thought it was going to rain.

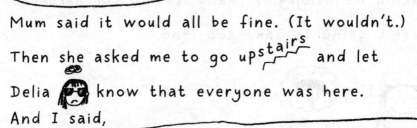

Mum said it would all be fine. (It wouldn't.) Then she asked me to go up stairs and let Delia know that everyone was here. And I said,

What's the point, she won't be pleased to see us.

W hich was true.

M um said, "Just go and knock on her door."

But I had a MUCH better idea than that.

I showed the cousins how to make some
paper bangers and
how to use them too.

Then we all took them upstairs and stood
outside Delia's bedroom door. I think using the
paper bangers to let Delia know that everyone
was here was a genius idea!

We flicked them over our heads, again ...

... and AGAIN...

BANG!

... and AGAIN...

BANG!

... and AGAIN...

Bang!

... and AGAIN...

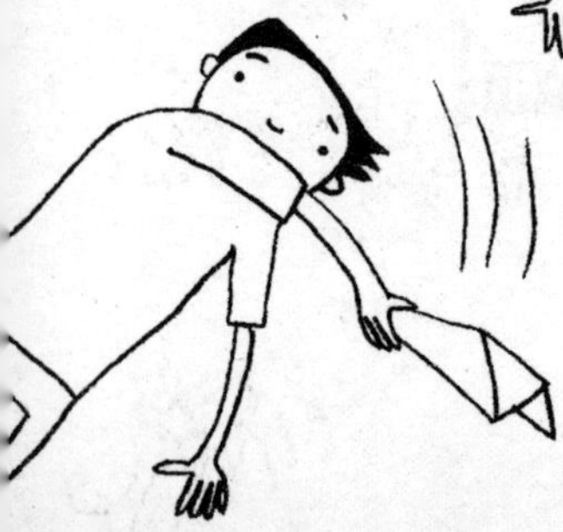

Bang!

(That was a good one!)

Delia came **storming out** of her room and told us to STOP being  (annoying little boys.)

So I told Delia that the cousins were | NOT | little and she was being rude.

Before Delia could get even more grumpy, Mum called upstairs and told us,

(The barbecue is nearly ready!)

I l⊙⊙ked out into the garden but all I could see was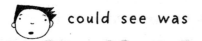

THiCK SMOKE EVErYwhere.

The smoke seemed to be getting

THICKER and thicker.

Mum had to rush round the whole house closing the windows to stop the SMOKE from coming in. I couldn't see Dad at all. I could only hear him calling from the smoke-filled garden for someone to...

Bring me a PLATE QUICKLY!

Turns out Uncle Kevin wasn't much help after all. He'd escaped back to the house because he said the smoke was getting in his eyes and he couldn't stop coughing.

cough

cough

Mum handed me a plate to give to Dad (which I did).

Eventually when the { smoke } died down, I could see that the sausages all looked a bit ...

OVERDONE?

Dad said it was important for barbecued meat to be cooked properly and I shouldn't worry.

They're fine.

I watched Dad turn the meat over and cook them a bit more. I'd never seen sausages that colour before. I asked Dad if the barbecue was ready yet.

And he said,  NEARLY.

And I said, "The sausages look a bit ... **burnt**, Dad?"

And Dad said "They're not burnt, they're just WELL DONE."

But when he tried to take the sausages off the barbecue and put them on the plate, they were ALL **stuck fast** to the nasty black **gunge** left on the grill. I reminded Dad that he said the **gunge** would burn off during cooking. And Dad told me I should go back to the house and find something more USEFUL to do.

Tell everyone that lunch is all under control.

(It wasn't.)

I left Dad scraping the sausages up while trying not to make too much of a mess on the plate.

Mum was trying to keep the smoke out of the kitchen with lots of tea-towel wafting. She asked me how everything was going.

I said, OK ... sort of. Which wasn't EXACTLY what Mum wanted to hear.

The cousins had taken my advice and eaten all the snacks.

Empty

BANG

BANG

Now they were playing with their paper bangers again.

I joined in and discovered that if I timed my paper banger SWING just right ...

NOISE

I couldn't hear a | word | Mum was saying.

"Sorry, Mum?"

BANG!

At least it took my mind off the burnt barbecue lunch that I knew was coming.

FINALLY Dad appeared through the SWIRLING smoke that was still hanging around

looking very pleased with himself and holding a nice BIG plate of (**burnt**) barbecued food. Well, he WAS holding a plate ... right up until I SWISHED the paper banger over my head and made a SPECTACULARLY LOUD...

BANG!

Dad was so STARTLED

he tripped ...

... which fell on the ground ...

and let go of the plate ...

along with all the food ...

... that got covered

in grass ... and loads of ants.

(Extreme close-up)

Yeah!

sausages

(Who were attracted by the black sticky gunge.)

And just when Dad thought that this barbecue couldn't possibly get any worse, it started to RAIN.

A lot.

Uncle Kevin's eyes got better just in
time for him to see all the burnt sausages
on the floor.
Dad blamed my paper banger for  guilty
making him drop the food,
while the cousins kept asking what was for
lunch now? hungry    Uncle Kevin said,

This is one **BIG** barbecue disaster!

Which was true but <u>not</u> very helpful (and it
really annoyed Dad).

I tried to make a suggestion but everyone was
distracted by ROOSTER
(Derek's dog).

Who suddenly JUMPED over the fence and snatched a sausage.

Dad suggested that he could put some more sausages on the barbecue as it was still hot? But Mum wasn't keen on that idea and neither was anyone else. Especially when the cousins pointed out how many ants were everywhere now.

Then Delia appeared and said,

Where's all the food?

Mum pointed to the ground, then to Rooster. Who was eating another sausage.

And THAT'S when I managed to

SAVE THE DAY ...

... by suggesting that maybe

It was the first time ALL day that anyone had really listened to me.

(Better late than never.)

The end.

There, now that's all done.

I'm about to do some more MONSTER doodling

when **Mr Fullerman**
SPOTS what I'm up to.

He announces to the class that if we're
finished, we should

"bring up our books to get them marked

straight away."

I give him my book - and
hope for the best. ☺

Well done, Tom.
Very good work.

5 merits

Keep this up and you'll be
in _NEXT MONTH'S_ newsletter
as well!

Mr Fullerman

I'd forgotten about my EXCELLENT*
DOODLE book cover being mentioned in the
NEWSLETTER - oh, and with the PHOTO
Mrs Mumble took too.

*See page 357 of Everything's Amazing (Sort Of)
for the whole story.

I'll have to get a few ExTRA copies and
leave them lying around the house so Mum
and Dad are reminded about my
good work and will say
nice stuff to me like,

Well done, Tom

while proudly showing
off the NEWSLETTER to
THE FOSSILS. Who might even
give me some extra

pocket money for being such a GOOD hard-
working grandson.

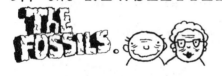

You're too kind, Granny.

Then Mum will
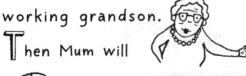 put the NEWSLETTER on the fridge.
(And if she doesn't, I will.) Which will annoy Delia

a lot.

I can't wait!

Mr Fullerman  says unfortunately this month's NEWSLETTER won't be ready to take home for a few reasons.

Photocopier ←

(a few reasons)

Luckily, I have other things to think about as well as my special mention in the NEWSLETTER. Like:

○ Who'll be picked to be a buddy?   Me? Maybe? Maybe not

○ More genius ideas that annoy Delia.

Guess who I am   Very funny

○ The NEW DOGZOMBIES video.

Me, Derek and Norman want to make our very own MUSIC video for DOGZOMBIES (our BAND). We watch DUDE3  music videos all the time so thought it would be AMAZING and fun to make our own. We've been talking about it for ages.

Let's do a video

Derek's dad says he can help us. Which is OK as long as he doesn't keep trying to **butt** in (like usual).

He's already been suggesting we watch a few more "classic music videos".

I'm here

no
no
no

What do you mean you've never seen "Sledgehammer"?

While I'm busy thinking of VIDEO ideas, **M**r **F**ullerman **surprises** me by saying...

"You too, TOM, ARMS UP!"

Because he keeps making us do EXTRA SPORTS DAY practices when we're least

expecting it.

Like now.

It's making it VERY

difficult to finish

off my LARGE doodle. And Marcus keeps on telling **M**r **F**ullerman when I'm drawing. (He's snitched quite a few times now.) Luckily for me, Marcus has been getting on **M**r **F**ullerman's nerves too. He tells Marcus to get on with his own work.

Sir

Which I agree with.  hummph

I've had to use ALL the excellent tricks I know to get this doodle finished.

Trick 1. Arranging books round me for cover. Always a good one. →

Trick 2. Looking straight ahead at the same time as drawing.

(Which takes a LOT of practice.)

Trick 3. Leaning over my work SO much Mr Fullerman

can't see what I'm doing. Like this... Which seems to be working. Even Marcus can't see.

I'm upside down

Yo!

WAFER TREE

(As it's MATHS tomorrow, I'll probably have to start a new one to keep me going.)

147

BUDDIES

? Today we get to find out about the buddies...

Oh, and there's maths too. 😦

(Doodle ideas ready if I get bored.)

It's not such a big deal if I don't get chosen.

I tell **AMY** she'll definitely get picked. And she says, "I'm not so sure."

So I say, "How can you say that?"

And she says, "Who'd pick me?"

I tell **AMY**, "You wouldn't want to pick an idiot, would you?"

"Thanks, Tom."

Brmmm

Brmmm

It's supposed to be a compliment, but from the way **AMY** said "Thanks, Tom" maybe it didn't sound like one.

Mr Fullerman is busy handing out letters about who's going to be a buddy and what they have to do.

Becoming a buddy

Being a buddy to some of the younger children is a very responsible role.
All buddies are expected to be: helpful, kind, good listeners with good advice.
Your teachers are there to help.
Remember to be the BEST buddy you can be!

Mr Keen

He tells the whole class, **"If you don't get chosen this time, you will have another chance next term."**

Then he hands a letter to ...

 and I say, "Told you!"

And then to ... ME!

Looks like I'm going to be a buddy to some kid in Class 2R?

Let me see who it is.

Joey Dawson.

That name rings a bell.

Marcus hasn't been chosen this time. He's peering over my shoulder to see who I've got.

He says, "Ha! Ha! That kid is trouble." And I say, "Well, I'm going to be a GOOD buddy and keep him out of trouble."

Then I remember who Joey Dawson is.

(I'm sure he's not like that ALL the time?)

Hooray, it's BREAK-TIME

I meet up with Derek and Norman, who have both been picked to be buddies. Derek says his buddy seems nice and Norman's buddy looks a bit like him (only smaller).

I can see Joey on the other side of the school grounds.

He's waving at me. I tell Derek and Norman that he's my buddy.

"Look, here he comes now."

We all watch Joey walk right through a game of football and not notice a thing. Which doesn't go down well with the other kids.

I want to make a good buddy impression, so
I say, "Thanks for choosing me as your buddy, Joey!"

Joey smiles but doesn't say anything.
I'm trying to remember what sort of stuff
is in the letter, and what I'm supposed to be
helping Joey with as his buddy.
I add...

"Got any worries about anything, Joey?"
He shakes his head no.
"Maybe school?"
Joey shakes his head again.
"Friends or teachers giving you a hard time?"
Joey shakes his head.

(This buddy business is going to be easy.)

Then I ask him,  "Have you got any questions you want to ask me?"

And Joey thinks for a bit ... and says, "Yes, can I be in your band, please?"

Which takes ALL of us by surprise.

Huh!

I wasn't expecting that question.

So I tell Joey that we're not looking for new band members right now.

"You can come to our next band practice and watch us if you want?"

Joey says, "That would be **great.**"

Then he jumps up and down and punches the air, saying, "YES! YES!" Which is funny!

...Until he accidentally

Mr Fullerman, who's walking past him on break duty. Mr Fullerman is NOT very happy because he's spilled his cup of tea as well.

He tells Joey, **"Joey, you must be more careful!"**

Then he adds, **"Tom, you're his buddy,** **you should be looking out for him."**

Like it was my fault! (It wasn't.)

Derek and Norman think it's a BAD idea to let Joey watch our band practice.

"He'll break something," Derek says.

"He's **worse** than **me**," Norman adds.

The band could definitely do with a practice and **another** gig.

The last time we played, it was for **Granny** Mavis and her Over **70s**

and Make Group. (Not sure it was a proper gig, though?) I promise Derek and Norman that if Joey turns up, I'll make sure he doesn't touch (or break) anything.

(Don't know how ... but I'll try.)

(Granny's Over 70s Cake & Make)

NEWSLETTER

and other interesting facts

Mr Keen, our headmaster (or **RED** master, as I call him when he gets **CROSS**), told us in assembly that the NEWSLETTERS have all been posted to our parents now.

"Along with some other important information AND your mid-term REPORT CARDS!"

I'm hoping that the GOOD mention in the NEWSLETTER will make up for anything **dodgy** that might be **LURKING** in my → REPORT CARD. (Fingers crossed there's no mention of made-up LATE NOTES or that kind of thing.)

Mrs Nap goes on to tell everybody about the SCHOOL TALENT-SHOW AUDITIONS. She says we are hoping to see "LOTS OF YOU TALENTED CHILDREN ALL COMING ALONG FOR THE AUDITIONS!"

Mrs Nap explains, "This year's production is a talent show, so anyone can join in. AND there will only be one dress rehearsal once you've been chosen, unlike last year's play."

Which is good to know.

I managed to avoid last year's PLAY -
unlike Solid.

(Solid as a tree. He was very good.)

Maybe **DOGZOMBIES** could be part of the show this year, especially with my **NEW GUITAR,** and because **DOGZOMBIES** can now play **SIX** whole songs all the way through. ♪ ♪ ♪

I can see it now...

Secret MESSAGES

(Shhhhh)

Back in class,

Mr **F**ullerman has found

yet another way of making

us do EXTRA practice for

SPORTS DAY. We all have to Jump up

and touch the arrow before he lets us come

into class.

Then he explains to the class what

we'll be doing today.

First of all, you need to write the WHOLE
alphabet out, and underneath each letter,
make up your own symbols. Remember
when we looked at the Egyptian
hieroglyphics?

That's what I want you all to do.

I thought it sounded a bit dull. Zzzzzzzz yawn yawn... I was getting ready to start a new doodle ... when M r Fullerman gave us some examples of a SECRET MESSAGE written in code.

We had to work out what the message said. It was BRILLIANT!

Crack the secret code below, then make up your OWN CODE for the alphabet.

A B C D E F G H I J K
L M N O P Q R S T U V
W X Y Z

Answer: HARD WORK

Next, we have to invent our OWN CODE.
Which could be VERY useful, especially if I
don't want certain people to know what
I'm writing about...

Marcus is LO**OO**KING
at what I'm doing and
SNIFFING right by my ear.

Nosy

? Sniff

I tell him to stop doing both and he says, "I'm
busy concentrating on my own code" (he's not).
His pen has started to leak and it's
leaving ink on his hands, which
he keeps puting on his face.
I try and tell him what he's doing.
But he ignores me and says Whatever.
(I did try.)

I spend the rest of the lesson making up my own

MONSTER ALiEN

code. Which I am VERY pleased with!

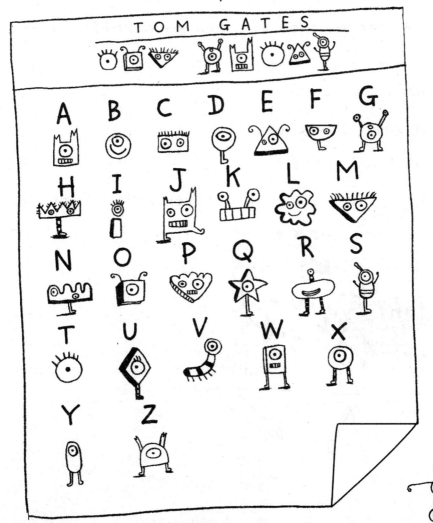

Once we've finished making up our own code, Mr Fullerman wants us to write a letter to the person sitting next to us. I write this one for Marcus, then pass him my ALPHABET so he can work out what it says.

It takes him a while.

Eventually he gets it.

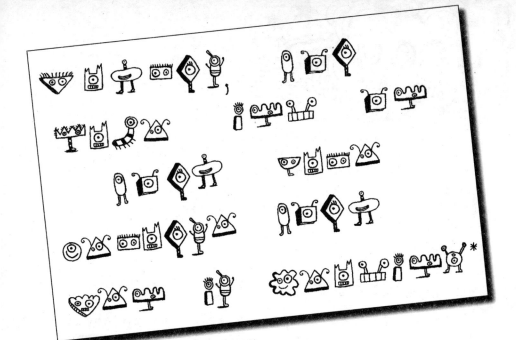

Ha! Ha!

*MARCUS, YOU HAVE INK ON YOUR FACE BECAUSE YOUR PEN IS LEAKING.

Buddy duties are proving to be trickier than I first thought. Every SINGLE break-time and lunchtime, Joey comes to say

Hello!

But that's ALL he says. (Joey doesn't talk much.) I tried to pass a few tips on about getting by in Oakfield School.

But it's hard to tell if he's interested or not.

Mr Fullerman is on break duty (again) and he's looking over in my direction. So I'm trying to show him that I'm being an excellent buddy.

168

I ask Joey if he'd like to have a game of
football with me and a few of my friends,

"Just a little kick around."
And Joey nods YES.

So I get a ball and ask Derek
and Solid to join in too. We're

kicking it to each other, nothing fancy.

Joey's actually pretty good at football. He's doing
OK. Mr Fullerman is still wandering around the
school grounds keeping an eye on everyone. And
(hopefully) noticing what a GOOD buddy I'm being.
I kick the football HIGH in the air and call out,
"Joey ... on your head!" And Joey jumps up
and tries to HEAD the ball back to me...

Well, I think that's what he wanted to do.

The ball FLIES off his head in the opposite direction and lands right in ... Mr Fullerman's cup of tea.

Which spills EVERYWHERE (again).

Mr Fullerman says,

"For GOODNESS' sake, Tom, will you LOOK where you're kicking that ball!"

And I want to shout, "It WASN'T ME!"

But because I am a NICE buddy, I say..."Sorry, sir."

Marcus has been watching us and comes over.

Joey

He says, "I'm glad I don't have a buddy like yours."

And I say, "It was an accident, wasn't it, Joey?"

But Joey's already gone back into school to avoid **M**r **F**ullerman and me (I think).

Marcus says, "I told you your buddy was trouble."

Thanks for that, Marcus.

On the way home from school, 🙂 Derek gets out **TWO** caramel wafers.

"My buddy gave them to me for being nice." And I'm thinking 😕 I DESERVE **LOADS** of WAFERS for [not] snitching on Joey. (Who's been staying out of my way since the football incident.)

Derek gives me one of his wafers, which is nice of him. I try and make mine last all the way home by eating it in sections.

Like this

Break in half

Eat in sections

I'm just finishing the last tiny little bit when I open the front door, go into the kitchen and find THIS PINNED UP ON THE FRIDGE!

OAKFIELD SCHOOL
NEWSLETTER

**DATES
FOR YOUR
DIARY**

ISSUE FOUR

WELL DONE
to **TOM GATES**
from Class 5F

For producing an
excellent piece of
homework -
fantastic drawings in
his sketchbook

NEW SCHOOL
MASCOT

Yes, Oakfield School
has a new visitor

CONGRATULATIONS!
to Adam and Zoe!
For a fabulous swim for Team Oakfield
and bringing back a medal

 My **HEAD** looks like a **GIANT**

PINEAPPLE.

(Shame.)

Mum says she is VERY pleased with me. But
we need to have a little **CHAT**  about
a few other things when Dad finishes work.

    (We do? That doesn't sound good.)

The only time Mum says things like that is if
I'm in trouble or if Delia has been blaming ME
for stuff I didn't do.

Who ate all the jam?

Empty

Jam

Tom did

Who used all the towels?

Tom did

Delia is upstairs LURKING around in the bathroom. I'm going to ask her what she's been saying about me NOW?

I wait for Delia to come out ...

... and when she does, I notice that her hair has turned a VERY odd colour.
It looks a bit ... green?

It IS GREEN!

I follow ══════▷ Delia into her room to get a PROPER look.

But she shuts the door and tells me to

GET LOST!

I ask her through the closed door, "What happened to your hair, Delia?"

And she tells me to

"Go AWAY, you're annoying."

So I say, "Did you know your hair's **GREEN?**"

Followed by,

"Why the **GREEN** hair?"

Delia says if I don't go away she'll tell Mum that I've been writing my own LATE NOTES How does she know that?

I go back to my room and while I'm  thinking of excuses in case Mum and Dad ask me about my late note ... I have a

GENIus iIDEA

for a song.

Which goes like this...
(As I've written down the words, it seems a shame not to do some nice drawings to go with it?)

Delia ... doesn't want to be SEEN

Because her hair has gone bright GREEN.

It looks the colour of a LEAF

Now Mum and Dad will give her GRIEF.

She tried to make her hair look FINE

But now it's gone a shade of LIME.

Delia ... she can be MEAN.
Delia ... her hair is GREEN.

I go back downstairs (still singing my new song) and Mum wants to know what I'm singing about.

Delia's GREEN hair.

Delia's clean hair?

And I say, No, green hair.

Then Dad comes in from his shed and CONGRATULATES me on being in the NEWSLETTER, then adds that we need to talk about a few other things too.

So I change the subject quickly and say, "Delia's got green hair."

Just then, **THE FOSSILS** (Granny Mavis and Granddad Bob) POP in to say "hello". Like they do. And Granny says, "Who's got **GREEN** hair?"

And I say, "Delia."

Granddad laughs and says, "At least she's got hair, not like me!"

Then I add, Or Dad. Which is true, but Dad doesn't look too happy now.

Mum goes upstairs to see Delia, and Dad says he's off to get changed.

Granny Mavis mentions she's taken up knitting again. She says, "I could make Delia a **HAT** if she needs one?"

Which is a GREAT idea.

May be I should help Granny with a few hat ideas.

Like these...

(This one is my personal favourite.)

Dad suddenly appears wearing →
THOSE shorts again.
He tells everyone "I'm going
for a brisk run," (like we wanted to know),

Then Mum comes back downstairs and says
that Delia's had a bit of a

HAIR-DYE DISASTER.

I say, "Really? I hadn't noticed." Mum says, "She's
probably been using some **TERRIBLE** cheap
hair dye. Rubbish hair DYE. Not like the one I use." FAB HAIR DYE

I tell Mum that Granny Mavis has
offered to knit Delia a hat.

"To cover up her green **hAIR**."

Mum says,

Actually, Delia's quite upset about her hair and doesn't want to see anyone because she's feeling a bit...

And I say, Like a tree?

Mum gives me a look and says,

No, Tom, she's feeling a bit self-conscious and embarrassed.

Granny says "Poor Delia" then tells us they're off to the shops to pick up a few odds and ends.

(From the look of Granny's list, it's mostly "odd" things.)

Buy ingredients for
sausage and jam rolls
peach and pea soup
Raspberry & tomato PIE

Then Mum says BYE to who wish her **LUCK** sorting everything out.

Mum WAS being all nice and sympathetic about Delia's hair.  Poor Delia

Right up until she discovered it [was] **HER** hair dye Delia had been using. Now she's really **NOT** happy about that!

FAB HAIR DYE

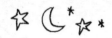

It's quite late when Dad gets back from his run. He looks **RED** in the face and is limping a bit. He says,

Puff Puff

"I'm in agony, I think I've pulled a muscle."

Mum asks, "Is that part of your carefully planned fitness regime too?"

Then she says, "At least you have an excuse not to run in the

PARENTS' RACE on Tom's SPORTS DAY."

How did she know about my SPORTS DAY? I've been keeping it quiet. Especially after last year's race.

Dad

Mr Fingle →

(Last year's race) →

I say, "You don't HAVE to come, my class are always **LAST** anyway."

Dad says he'll be **fine** and he's looking forward to running and **BEATING** Derek's dad this time. (I'm not.)

Mum wants to know if I'm auditioning for the school talent show tomorrow as well?

How does she know about that?

"I read your **NEWSLETTER** and your mid-term→ REPORT CARD too."

Oh! Oh! My report card has arrived.

Dad says, Which reminds me, we want to talk to you about your report card, Tom.

(I'm getting worried now.)

Dad limps over to get it. I can't remember anything **BAD** that I've done (apart from the LATE NOTE and a few other notes too).

Mum and Dad are both looking at me with very serious faces. They say, "Tom, we are very surprised that..."

You are an idiot

"You're doing **SO WELL!** It's amazing. Well done! Keep it **UP!**"

WOW! That's a first for me. My report card usually says things like:

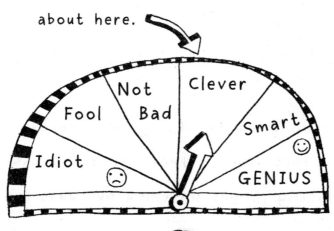

Tom does too much chatting/doodling.

Tom doesn't do enough homework/ maths.

But [now] on a scale of Idiot to Genius I'm about here.

Idiot ☹ Fool Not Bad Clever Smart ☺ GENIUS

Mum thinks I should put my guitar to good use and enter **DOGZOMBIES** in the talent show. "You're doing so well at everything!"

Good point. Maybe we could do it?

I give **N**orman a ring first and then **D**erek to see if they agree.

Let's!

Yeah

They do.

While I'm on the phone to Derek, I remind him about last year's parents' race and how embarrassing it was watching our dads run.

Then I have a **Terrible** thought.
"Cycling shorts ... my dad could turn up
wearing those cycling shorts!"

Derek says,

Shame.

While we're chatting on the phone,
I can  hear Rooster in Derek's
garden running around

barking like MAD. Derek says
Rooster's been chewing all his socks,
which is driving him **BONKERS.**
And I suddenly think of an excellent way to
avoid a possible SPORTS DAY cycling
shorts shame after all.

(Genius idea. 💡)

SPORTS DAY!

Now Dad's cycling shorts have miraculously disappeared, I'm fine with him and Mum both coming to my SPORTS DAY.

I'd better remember to bring ALL my own sports kit (for good reason). On the way to school, Derek tells me that his dad has actually been *practising for the parents' race.*

Wear this

He has? Wow, that's embarrassing.

Before we go to the sports ground, Mr Fullerman gives the whole class what he calls a

motivational talk.

His eyes look even **bigger** than usual because he is all enthusiastic.

GO FOR IT, CLASS 5F! TRY YOUR BEST AND HAVE FUN.

I say to AMY,

"What he really means is ... don't be rubbish and come last again."

Which is true.

The sports grounds are divided up into sections for all the different "sports" we'll be doing. Mrs Worthington RINGS a big BELL to start off each "sport" or race. Every class gets points for:

Goals scored

Beanbags caught

Balls bounced

Long jumps taken

Hulas hooped

When all the classes have done every "sport", the points are added up and the **WINNERS** are announced – after the parents' race, of course.

Mr Sprocket's class are wearing vests with **SLOGANS** on so they look like a proper team.

We just look like ... Class 5F.
Mrs Worthington rings the bell to begin the first session.

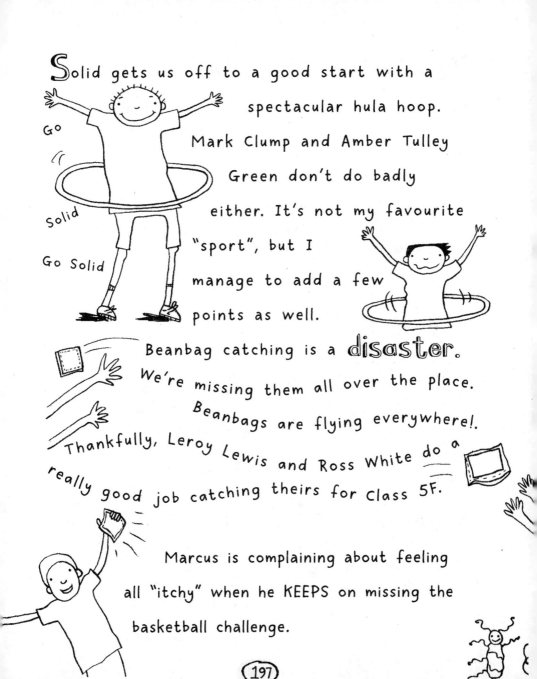

Solid gets us off to a good start with a spectacular hula hoop. Mark Clump and Amber Tulley Green don't do badly either. It's not my favourite "sport", but I manage to add a few points as well.

Go

((

Solid

Go Solid

Beanbag catching is a **disaster.** We're missing them all over the place. Beanbags are flying everywhere! Thankfully, Leroy Lewis and Ross White do a really good job catching theirs for Class 5F.

Marcus is complaining about feeling all "itchy" when he KEEPS on missing the basketball challenge.

And he blames me for *shoving* him, which I did (accidentally).

Mr Fullerman seems to be smiling, which is better than **last year.**

Oh well

AMY and Indrani are telling Julia that she's doing really well and not to be nervous about the long jump, which is our last sport.

It's not helping that Mr Sprocket is leading his class in a LOUD...

Give me a **W**

Give me an **I**

Give me an **N**

Give me another **N**

Give me an **E**

Give me an **R**

Give me an **S**

What have you got?

There's a slight pause as none of the class can work out what they've just spelled. In the end it's **Mr Fullerman** who says...

"It spells WINNERS, but don't count on it"

to Mr Sprocket's class.

Mr Fullerman's **EXTRA** SPORTS DAY  training starts paying off, as we're doing very well in the beanbag relay race.

Mr Keen is wandering around saying encouraging things like:

"Perfect pass, Pansy" and

"Really fast run, Robert."

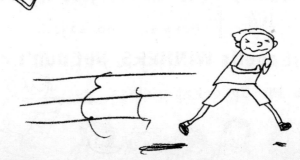

There are lots of families, friends and parents on one side of the grounds behind a barrier who are *cheering* too.

I can't see 👁️ 👁️ anyone from my family ... yet. Mrs Worthington rings the bell for everyone to stop for:

Drinks, oranges and BISCUITS.

Which is VERY popular.
During the break, Mr Fullerman tells us that everyone is doing BRILLIANTLY and we're definitely NOT going to come last this year.

Yes! Yes!

(I think he's more pleased than we are.)

Norman has somehow managed to eat WAY too many biscuits. And as the sugar starts to kick in, he's rolling around on the ground with his legs in the air saying...

Look, I'm a dying fly!

"Yes, you are, Norman."

(Oh dear.)

The last sport for Class is the **long** jump. I still can't see any of my family in the crowd at all. Until **AMY** says,

 You're popular.

I glance over to where Amy's looking.

Now I can see ...

... AND HEAR them.

(Shame.)

$\mathbb{I}$ manage to get **THE FOSSILS** not to wave the

WE LOVE YOU, TOM banner.

$\mathbb{L}$uckily, I'm not the only one with an embarrassing family. Julia Morton's parents are wearing $\mathbb{T}$-shirts ...

 with her  FACE on them.

$\mathbb{W}$hich hasn't helped her feel any less **NERVOUS**.

$\mathbb{M}$rs Worthington rings the

 bell and says, *"It's time for the last sport. GOOD luck!"*

Which is LONG JUMP in our case.
I take my turn ... *run* as
fast as I can and ...

...throw myself into the sand pit. Yes

It's not a bad j u m p either.
Good enough for THE FOSSILS to take out
the WE LOVE YOU, TOM banner again.

Yeah

Most of the class have jumped and there's just TWO kids to go.

Mr Fullerman (who's been having a sneaky peek ⊂⊃ ⊂⊃ at the scores) says,

**Only a few points between
Mr Sprocket's class and us now.**

Which is good news.

 The last TWO jumps need to be as LONG as POSSIBLE!

Julia Morton and Marcus say OK

But I'm not sure they're feeling confident.

Marcus goes first. The class start clapping to help him jump further. When he starts running, they all say...

"Whhhhhooooooooooooooooo!"

until he lands.

Then it's an, "Oooooooh?" as his long jump is ... only a tiny bit better than last time.

Itchy →

Marcus says he got distracted in mid-air by his ITCHY T-shirt. (If you say so, Marcus.)

Then Julia goes to jump.
She looks very NERVOUS.

The class go...

Whhhhhoooo

oooo!

Yeah! very long jump

Because Julia's jump is AMAZING! We're all cheering and clapping. But we won't know who's won the SPORTS DAY trophy until after the parents' races.
(I'd forgotten about that)

Just like last year, some dads are taking the race a LOT more seriously than others.

My dad is trying to pretend the race is

Just a bit of FUN.

But from the Determined LOOK on his face and the fancy running shoes he's wearing, I can tell he wants to WIN.

Mrs Worthington sets them off with a whistle ≡3 this time.

Fancy trainers

Dad manages to **HUFF** and _PUFF_ himself into ...

THIRD PLACE!

(Embarrassing headband)

PUFF

YES!

Ahead of Derek's dad (Mr Fingle), which he is VERY pleased about.

I say to Derek, "Phew, over for another year!" And Derek says, "I can't believe my dad wore that headband."

(I'm guessing Rooster might have something else to play with later.)

Mum says she can't run in the "mums' race" because she's worn the wrong shoes (accidentally on purpose, I think).

whoops!

Now the THE FOSSILS want to know why there isn't a grandparents' race too? (I'm sort of glad there isn't, to be honest.)

M_r K_{een} comes over and says they have added up **ALL** the points and are ready to announce the

"**winner of this year's**
SPORTS DAY **Trophy, who is ...**

Class 5N!"

It's Mrs Nap's class ... and we're SECOND. In front of Mr Sprocket's class. But from the way Mr Fullerman is leaping around and

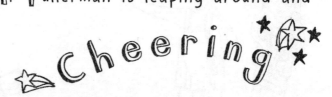

Cheering

you'd think it was us who had won.

I've never seen him so happy.

The VERY **best** thing about coming **second** at SPORTS DAY is that Mr Fullerman is in an EXCELLENT ☐ mood ☐ ☺ for the rest of the week.

He has made a special SPORTS DAY DISPLAY, which is ...

SECOND 5F THIRD 5S

Sports Day was won this year by 5N

Everyone who took part had a fantastic time. Especially 5F and Mr Fullerman.

SECOND WERE CLASS 5F

... right outside Mr Sprocket's classroom.

**Sports Day
Winners 5N**

The morning of the auditions for the school **Talent Show**

I'm a bit achy after SPORTS DAY. (All that jumping into sandpits and catching beanbags.)

On the way to school Derek and I discuss the audition and what song we should play. Derek says it  has to be "Smoke on the Water".

And I say, Why's that? And Derek says, "Because the old folks loved that song and Mrs Nap and Mr Sprocket are quite old so they'll like it too."

Good point. ➡️

"Smoke on the Water"
Old folks enjoying the song

I've brought my new guitar to school. And I'm a bit nervous that something might happen to it. I get even more worried when the first person we see is ...

Joey.

He's not been around much since the football incident. But because I am a GOOD buddy, I say, (Hi, Joey) and tell him we're auditioning for the school talent show.

He says, (I'll see you there.)

He will?

Straight away I'm thinking, I'll have to keep an EXTRA eye on my guitar. I don't want anything happening to it with Joey around.

In class, I ask **Mr Fullerman** if he could keep his beady eyes (•)(•) on my guitar until it's time for the auditions. I don't ask him like THAT.

Obviously.

Please, Mr Fullerman, could you keep my guitar in a safe place?

AMY, Indrani and Florence are all singing for their audition. I ask Marcus what he's doing and he says,

"A magic act that I've been practising a LOT. So it's really good."

And I say,  Can you do any magic now?

And he says [no] because he needs his special [box] of magic tricks.
Which sounds interesting.

I tell Marcus that my granddad taught me how to do a really good

 and I can show

him if he wants?

Marcus says,

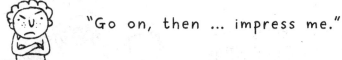 "Go on, then ... impress me."

MY GRANDDAD'S MAGIC TRICK

Empty

Granddad's trick goes like this...

1. Take a tissue and **scrunch** it up in your hand, then say *I can make it* **disappear.**

2. Then stand up and hold the tissue in your hand. Move your hand up and down while counting to four like this.

One...   Two...   Three...

Four...

3. Then on the fourth or fifth time, LET GO of the tissue by throwing it | behind | the person's head so they don't see it.

Now open your hand really slowly to show that the tissue has DISAPPEARED.

It does take a bit of practice.

Gone

But it worked really well on Marcus.

School Talent Show AUDITIONS

Joey comes to our classroom to collect us for our audition because he is helping Mr Sprocket.

I hold on to my guitar tightly and say, "Hi, Joey." He nods hello.

Ready?

We're walking to the hall when Norman says, " are definitely coming to play here because the whole school are talking about it."

And I say, "I hope it's TRUE, Norman. It would be SO good."

(Rumours often start in school that aren't true.)

Aliens have landed in the playground...

Really?

Rumour in school

Frisbee →

What really happened

Derek is already waiting for us along with Marcus (who's auditioning next).

Marcus is wearing ... a CAPE.

He's swishing it around and trying to be all dramatic.

Swish

Mr Sprocket calls out,

DOGZOMBIES NEXT, PLEASE.

But before we can start, Mr Sprocket asks for help

carrying some chairs and checking the drum kit is at the right height first, please.

We have no choice.

Just prop your guitar over there for a second, Tom.

I'm NOT going to do THAT! So Joey offers to hold it. And I have to stop myself from saying,

NO WAY!

Then MARCUS says, I'll look after it. Which is only a tiny bit better than Joey, but I don't have much of a choice. So while we go with Mr Sprocket to pick up the chairs and a few music stands, Marcus is left holding my guitar. Like this... ➡

I can see 👀 him FIDDLING with the strings! I tell him, "Don't touch the strings." But he ignores me. Now he's TWIDDLING with the end of my guitar and doing ROCK STAR poses while pretending to play it. I can't take my guitar back FAST enough!

Marcus says, "Don't snatch."
Guitar in hand – we get ready for our audition.

Hello – we're **DOGZOMBIES**.

But when I start to play "SMOKE ON THE WATER", it doesn't sound like "Smoke on the Water". It sounds **TERRIBLE**.

My guitar has gone out of tune because Marcus was fiddling **SO MUCH** with the strings. I have to keep going.

But it's a rotten audition. I can tell from the faces Mr Sprocket and Mrs Nap are pulling. They look like they're in pain.

When we've finished, Mr Sprocket says,

Well done. Just a few tuning issues to be sorted out ... but not bad, boys.

Which is better than I thought. Derek tells me not to worry. Norman says, It wasn't so bad.

Marcus says, "What happened? You lot were RUBBISH! More like DOG'S DINNER than DOGZOMBIES."

Which is irritating ... but true.

Derek says, "Thanks, Marcus. Let's see how YOU do, then?" Marcus SWISHES his cape and goes off to perform.

He announces himself as **"MAGIC MARCUS"**.

Which sounds like MAGIC MARKERS and makes us all **LAUGH**. Ha! Ha! Ha!

Marcus is doing tricks with cards and all kinds of different things and is surprisingly good, which is a bit annoying.

Now Joey has brought along **AMY**, Florence and Indrani for their audition.

"How did you do?" Amy asks me.

I was about to say,
"Not bad ... or OK, but might have done
better" when Joey decides to BUTT in and
tells AMY,

They were TERRIBLE, all out of tune.

Thanks, Joey! He's normally quiet. Some buddy
he turned out to be. It wasn't my fault the
guitar went out of tune.

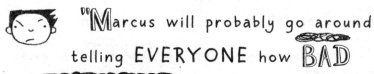 I tell Derek and Norman that "Marcus will probably go around telling EVERYONE how **BAD** **DOGZOMBIES** were."

And Derek says, Do you think so?

Yes, that's EXACTLY what Marcus does.

Hopeless, they were

Shame

It was painful to listen to

DOGZOMBIES were RUBBISH

Oh dear

Now ALL the **school** are talking about **DUDE3** playing at the school talent show. **AND** the RUBBISH audition **DOGZOMBIES** did.

Which was THE **WORST** audition **EVER** in the **WHOLE** **HISTORY** of the school.

(That last bit's not true ... but that's what it FEELS like everyone is saying.)

It's `not` very long before the list of successful AUDITIONS gets pinned up on the school notice board. Somehow ... **DOGZOMBIES** has made it.

Oakfield School Talent Show Audition Results

If your name is below, you're in the SHOW!

We'll have ONE dress rehearsal before the show.

Well done, EVERYONE

Brad Galloway	Indrani Hindle
Julia Morton	Florence Mitchell
Minnie Verner	Paul Rogers
June Rawlings	Jenny Chan
Tom Gates	Christina Brown
Norman Watson	Roger Wood
Derek Fingle	Emily Border
Marcus Meldrew	Chad Dury
Amy Porter	Paul Jolly

SPECIAL GUEST APPEARANCE TO BE ANNOUNCED

In fact, looking at the list, I think everyone who auditioned made it.

Right at the bottom it says

SPECIAL GUEST APPEARANCE

to be announced.

Which looks interesting?

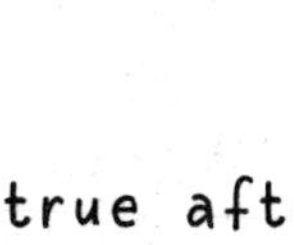

Could the RUMOURS be true after all?

Family Outing to the CINEMA

On the way home we _BUMP_ into Joey going the other way.

(When I say we bumped into him ... I mean we _BUMPED_ into him.)

I ask him if he's **OK?**

He nods. Then he says,

When can I come to your band practice?

I'd forgotten about that.

And I'm looking at Derek, who seems a bit alarmed.

$\mathbb{I}$ tell Joey that we're SUPPOSED to be filming our BAND [VIDEO] soon.

It might not be a good time to come and watch us. Sorry.

$\mathbb{J}$oey says,  I could come and help you and bring WAFERS.

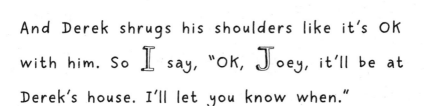

And Derek shrugs his shoulders like it's OK with him. So $\mathbb{I}$ say, "OK, $\mathbb{J}$oey, it'll be at Derek's house. I'll let you know when."

Joey says, "Yeah, thanks." Then he runs off and bumps into someone else coming around the corner.

AGH! Whoops

When I get home Mum reminds me

that we're supposed to be having some

 QUALITY family time together tonight.

And I say, We are?

"Yes, we're going to the cinema. We have to go somewhere dark or Delia won't come with us while her hair's still a bit GREEN."

"What are we seeing?"

Mum says it's a great film that's had lots of good reviews.

 "It's called The tter."

And I say, "What's it about?"
Because I've never heard of the film?
Then Delia butts in and she says,

"It's about an OTTER, stupid."

So I say, "Not necessarily, it could be a
film about SPIES and
'THE OTTER' is a code name for a secret agent."
And Delia says,
"OR it could be about an OTTER and
that's why there's a MASSIVE
picture on the film poster of AN OTTER."

Mum says,
"All right, Delia,
that's enough."

Then I suggest that if Delia doesn't want to be seen with her GREEN hair, she could always ask Granny Mavis to knit one of these hats for her?

 Like this or this.  Then Dad comes in and says,

> Has anyone seen my cycling shorts? I can't find them any where.

This seems like a good time to disappear to my room and wait until we're all ready to go.

Which takes AGES.

WAIT! I forgot my glasses
Groan

We're so late we nearly miss the start of the film. As we're buying the tickets, Mum is getting STRESSED because she likes to sit near the FRONT of the cinema and she's worried it will all be FULL. And she HATES it when people eat too LOUDLY. Mum thinks there should be RULES for what you can eat in the cinema.

Crunch
Munch
Slurp

I've brought a few fruit chews that I unwrap BEFORE the film starts. Otherwise Mum will keep STARING and nudging me until I stop.

We all manage to get seats near the front before the film starts. Delia has got her hood up and looks even more grumpy than usual. I tell Dad that I don't want to sit next to her if she's taking off her sunglasses again.

Grump

So Dad sits between us.

We're all settled and the lights are just going down. Mum's happy with her seat. There's no one eating too LOUDLY near us. Everything is great. When this happens to me...

I can't see a thing now!

That's just great. I keep moving from side to side but I still can't see the film. Mum tells me to stop fidgeting, Tom.

SWAPPED

I say, "I can't see." So Mum swaps seats with me. And for about a minute I can see the whole screen.

Then the TALLEST man in the world with the BIGGEST head does this ... and that's when I realize who's sitting in front of me.

It's Solid and HIS DAD.

I tap him on the back
and say, "Hi!" And
Mum says, "Shhhhhhh."

I decide to go and sit next to him because I can't see anything behind him or his dad.

The film is REALLY Funny. Even Delia is laughing (but I'm not going to look at her without her glasses again).

Mum keeps tapping me on the head every time Solid and I chat. Even a tiny bit.

Solid says, "Are your whole family here?"

And I whisper,

"Yes, we're having quality family time watching a film. So we don't have to talk to each other."

Then Mum Taps me on the head again and tells me to... Shhhhhhhhhh...

Groan

When the film is finished, Dad says he's going to the toilet and he'll meet us outside. We all get up to leave and Solid and I are **chatting** about the film, our SPORTS DAY and the school auditions, STUFF like that.

It's only when he says BYE and walks off with his dad that I realize how similar they both are.

Solid

His dad

Mum wants to know what's taking Dad so long and she goes off to find him, leaving me outside with Delia (who's getting grumpier).

Then suddenly Delia *Huh!* notices that Ed, her old boyfriend, is coming out of the cinema with some of his friends. She tells me, "Don't move or ELSE." And ducks behind me.

I decide to have some fun and start moving from side to side so Delia has to follow me. I can hear Delia whispering behind me, "Don't you DARE" as Ed looks up and sees me. I wave and say, "Hi, Ed, fancy seeing you here."

Ed comes over and says, "Hi, Tom." And I say, "Good film, wasn't it?" and he says, "Great ... are you still in your band?"

Ａnd I say, "Yes, thanks."

Delia's still crouched down with her hood covering her GREEN hair and she's trying to sneak away without Ed noticing. Which might have worked if I hadn't moved out of the way at exactly the same time as a

BIG gust of wind SWEEPS Delia's hood right off her head. Delia's GREEN hair stands out a LOT.

E veryone is looking at her – including Ed.
M um and D ad come back just in time to
stop Delia from taking her **REVENGE**
on me. She says, "You wait."

Which doesn't sound good.

So I suggest Delia lightens up
and has some FUN. "Like me!"
Mum says it's nice that we're
both enjoying ourselves.
(Well, I am... Delia looks a bit grumpy and
GREEN still.)

With all the stuff that's been going on in school, it's easy to forget about my...

Homework?

Because Mr Fullerman is STILL in a super good mood from SPORTS DAY, he says I can bring it in tomorrow. Which is good news for me.

I've been spending LOADS of my time at home (and in class) PLANNING and thinking of ideas for the DOGZOMBIES VIDEO.

Planning for the video

There are SO many things we could do. Like:

○ Make **WiLD THiNG** masks.

○ Make **WILD THING** posters to put in the background.

○ Film in the garden, which looks a bit jungley in parts.

I've got **LOADS** of IDEAS going on in my head. And writing a WHOLE A4 page about "MY SPORTS DAY" just isn't one of them.

"Tomorrow" has come round a bit **too** quickly  - I've only managed to write a bit of my homework while on the way to school this morning.

I have to finish it off under my desk ... and on my lap ... so **Mr Fullerman** can't see what I'm doing.

Under the circumstances I think I've done OK?

My Sports Day

By TOM GATES

I REALLY LIKED SPORTS DAY THIS YEAR BECAUSE WE NEARLY WON! YEAH! AND MR FULLERMAN HAS BEEN IN A GOOD MOOD.

WE HAD NICE ORANGE BISCUITS, WHICH WAS A TREAT. YEAH!

Tom ....

Y o u   s   e   e   m

t   o   b   e

s   p   a   c   i   n   g

o   u   t   your words a lot?

This does not fool me into thinking

you have done a whole A4 page!

Don't try this again.

Mr Fullerman

Phew ... could have been worse.

No detention or mention of "EXTRA WORK".

DOGZOMBIES VIDEO

After an **EXHAUSTING** week at school, me, Norman and Derek are very busy making some important decisions about the **DOGZOMBIES** video that we're filming today.

1. Hats or  no hats?

2. Sunglasses or no sunglasses?

3. Outside or ☼ inside?

4. Masks or  no masks?

5. Wafers now or later? Cool!

Wafers later is the only decision we've made so far. Mostly because we don't want Norman to peak too soon.

I say, "What do you think  would do if they were making this video?" Derek says he doesn't think they'd wear masks.

It's a good point. We stick to the **DOGZOMBIES** T-shirts instead and film inside Derek's garage, as it looks like it might rain. Mr Fingle has offered to help out and has set up the camera on his fancy TRIpod. Which is great. But it does mean we can't move around much or we won't be in shot.

Derek's dad starts talking about classic music videos of our time.

AGAIN.

So Derek has to remind him that we're just doing this for fun. We're saved when Mr Fingle's phone rings – which keeps him busy for a bit. Derek says, "Shall we just press play on the camera and have a go then?"

It's a good plan. But we can't work out who's going to do it, because it's tricky pressing play, then running back into shot. We're just about to start filming when this time MRS Fingle comes in! She says, "You have a visitor to see DOGZOMBIES!" We do?

(259)

 Hello

It's Joey.

Who I invited round to watch us

do a band practice ... and then

forgot all about. Come round tomorrow

OK

Joey says his mum will

be picking him up in two hours.

And Derek says,

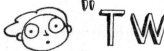 "TWO HOURS!"

like it's a really really long time. Then Joey

shows us a very small cool camera that his

mum has lent him to use today. "I can do

some filming too if you want?"

Which is an excellent idea.

(Joey's turning out to be really helpful after all.)

Though J oey does *knock* the tripod over twice.

M r Fingle comes back and starts making a few filming suggestions.

S ome are better than others...

Stand on one leg ... then PLAY!

Really?

But it does make TWO HOURS *WHIZZ* by.

J oey's mum turns up just as we're really getting into filming. She says, "This looks good! I'll help you put the video together if you want."

Joey's
mum →

Norman says, "SWEET."

(He means that's good.)

Then Joey says, "That reminds me - I brought you these."

He throws me a whole pack of

caramel WAFERS!

YEAH! Then knocks over the camera for the THIRD time.

Camera!

Mr Fingle's checking his camera's still working (it is). I'm thinking Joey has turned out to be an excellent buddy after all.

Bye!

rehearsal

Mr Fullerman

reminds us that there's a

"RUN-THROUGH today for the school talent show before the REAL show, which is ... tonight."

I whisper to **AMY**, 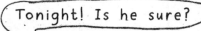 Tonight! Is he sure?

 And **Mr Fullerman** says, **"Yes, Tom, tonight."**

How could I have forgotten when the school production was?

TALENT SHOW is THIS THURSDAY. DON'T FORGET!

SCHOOL NOTICE BOARD

TALENT

TALENT SHOW TONIGHT
Special Guests

The GOOD news is DOGZOMBIES rehearsal time is at 11:15. It looks like I'll be missing ... MATHS. ☺

Result! (Making the DOGZOMBIES video was a bit of extra practice for us too, which is good.)

Marcus has his run-through before us at eleven o'clock. He's sitting next to me complaining (as usual). He thinks he should be on last. And I say, "How do you work that one out, Marcus?" and he says, "Because my act is the best one." And I say, "It might not be?"

And he says, "No one else is doing magic tricks like me."

And I say, "What about the

SPECIAL GUESTS?

There's a **RUMOUR** that **DUDE 3** are coming to our school. They're better than you."

And he says, "Don't be **STUPID** ... **DUDE 3** won't come to our school. That's not going to happen, is it?"

Then he starts **SCRATCHING** his back, which makes ME feel itchy too. I stop scratching when I notice **AMY**, Indrani and Florence are looking at me.

They are getting ready to sing after **DOGZOMBIES**, followed by Mark Clump.

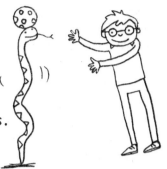

Who apparently is bringing in one of his **pets** that he's trained to do tricks.

(Maybe his snake? Which would be impressive.) Brad is doing street dancing (not behind **Mr Fullerman's** back this time either).

I *wish* I knew who the

SPECIAL GUESTS were!

If it's NOT **DUDE 3** ... who can it be? Mr Sprocket and Mrs Nap are not saying a word at the run-through.

They tell me...
"You'll have to wait and see like everyone else, Tom."
Which is **irritating**. Because I wanted to go home and tell **D**elia that

DUDE 3 were coming to our concert tonight.

She's not going out much because of her (slightly) **GREEN** hair.

But it would still annoy her to miss them.

And I would remind her how she'd missed them ... a lot.

Ha!

Oh well ... it can't be **DUDE 3**, can it?

Norman **MUST** have got that wrong.

At lunchtime Joey comes to find me and he says he's got a finished film of us playing "**WILD THING**".

"I'll ask my mum to send it to you, it's really good." ☺

(I am a **GENIUS** for getting Joey as a buddy – OK, I know he picked me, but it's still worked out well.)

High five

Because of the school production, everybody is allowed to go home an hour earlier to get ready.

Which doesn't take me and Derek long to do.

BEFORE

AFTER

Derek is round at my house and we're looking at some copies of **ROCK WEEKLY** when I suggest that if we're going to look more like a **ROCK** band, I should wear some "shades

or **SPIKE** up my hair ... like this?"

And he says, "Do you think so?"
It might be a good idea."

I go into the bathroom and
help myself to some hair gel
that's been there for a while.
I think Uncle Kevin bought
it as a present for Dad ... as
a **joke.**

I still have a selection
of Delia's
sunglasses that we can
"borrow" for tonight, which both Derek and I
think we look pretty good in.

Derek stays at mine for some dinner and while we're eating, Dad comes in holding a plastic bag. He says, "I've got myself some new shorts for running."

Which he's pleased about.

I whisper to Derek, "Let's hope Rooster's still hungry." Which makes him laugh.

TALENT → SHOW TONIGHT

(PLUS SPECIAL GUESTS!)

Chat
Chat

All the kids that are performing tonight are getting ready in the classrooms near the hall. There's a **lot** of excited chatting going on before the show starts. Me, Derek and Norman are all wearing our **DOGZOMBIES** T-shirts.

I show Norman the hair gel and say, "I think I should spike up my hair to look cooler and more like a

ROCK STAR"

And **AMY**, who's with Florence, hears me and says, "You should do it, Tom! That would look really good!" Norman just says,

YEAH!

because he's already getting a bit twitchy (like he does).

So I get a big handful of hair gel and put it in my hair, where it stays in a big

BLOB.

Derek says, "I think you need to rub it in a bit."

Which I do. "What now?"

 AMY and Florence are looking at my hair. Florence says, "Maybe you should spike it up using a brush?" But I don't have one. **AMY** says I can borrow her brush, which is nice of her. Now I've got half a

 of hair gel in my hair, I must look a bit silly.

Derek suggests I

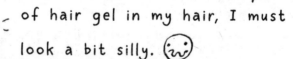
go and find a mirror so you can see what you're doing.

(Good thinking.) I head to the toilet and try to SPIKE up my hair using **AMY**'s funny little round brush.

I've never used one of these before.

I twiddle it round the front of my hair, then try and drag it up^{wards} into a SPIKE.

But it's STUCK. So I twist it round a bit more. Which doesn't work at all. This is NOT good. I'm trying not to PANIC. But the more I twist the brush, the more tangled up it gets.

This is turning out to be a DISASTER!

  I'm taking so long that Derek comes to find me.

He says, "We need to get ready now, Tom." And I say, "There's a tiny bit of a problem."

And Derek says, "I know, Mr Sprocket  wants us to go on early because of Marcus."

I don't think Derek has realized that the brush I'm holding in my hand is actually STUCK. I keep trying to get the brush out while asking,

"What's the problem with Marcus?"

Derek says, "Mr Sprocket wants us to perform $FIRST$ because Marcus has got..."

 I say,

"Nervous? ... Cold feet? ...

More annoying than ever?"

Derek says,

"No, not quite. He's cancelled because he's

got..."

"A bit of a **RASH**."

(Marcus scratching.)

Derek tells me his mum called and said it's not serious, but Marcus says he can't do his tricks because he's all ITCHY.

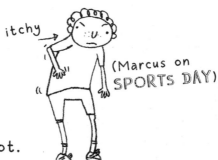

itchy →

(Marcus on SPORTS DAY)

That explains a lot.

Finally, Derek notices the brush sticking out of the top of my hair.

"What's wrong with your hair, Tom?"

"The brush is stuck,"

I say.

Derek has a go at trying to pull the brush out. I say "AGHHHH!"

so he stops.

281

"How did you do THAT?"

"I twisted the brush and now it's stuck ... the hair gel made it worse."

I need to get help ... FAST!

But no one knows what to do.

Not even Mr Sprocket or Mrs Nap can get the brush out of my hair.

Mrs Mumble comes over. She says, "Joey got a comb stuck JUST like that."

"How did you get the comb out, Mrs Mumble?"
Mrs Mumble makes a scissor-cutting

movement with her fingers.

"His mum had to cut the comb out.

It was the only way, I'm afraid."

That's just great, then. GROAN...

Mr Sprocket says that we can go

on later if I need the time to sort out the

brush.

I say, "YES – we need LOADS more time."

(Like a WEEK.)

Mr Sprocket says I will have to get my mum

or dad to help now. Derek says he could go

and look for my mum in the audience if I

want.

"They should be here by now?"

Reluctantly, I say OK.

Mum takes one look at me and the brush and says, "How did you manage to do that, Tom?" I say, "It's a mystery, I just brushed my hair." (I don't mention the half ton of hair gel.)

AMY is feeling a bit guilty because it was her idea to use the brush.

She says, "I don't need it back if you have to BREAK it."

I really hope Mum's not going to do THAT!

Hi ya!

But the only pair of scissors that anyone can find to cut my hair with are a bit **BLUNT,** with round tips that are meant for paper.

 Mum says, "I CAN'T use those, Tom."

So I have to either:

o   Ignore the brush (bit tricky).

o   Wear a BIG hat.

o   Wear a mask.

I don't want to go on stage with this brush **BOUNCING** around on my head.

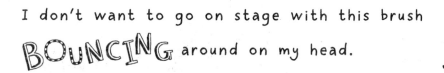

The TALENT show has already started and seems to be going OK without Marcus.

Mr Keen made an announcement that there might be a few changes to the running order of the show.

We're now going to play LAST, so I'm hoping my hairbrush problem will be ALL sorted by then.

Ta da!

But it's not looking good.

Norman and Derek are shaking their heads and staring at me.

"This isn't working, is it, Tom?" Derek says.

He's right.

I don't want to go and play "**WILD THING**" in front of the school with a BRUSH sticking out of my hair.

I tell Mr Sprocket and Mrs Nap that I'm REALLY sorry, but I won't be able to play now.

"Never mind, Tom, We'll get the SPECIAL GUESTS to go on earlier," Mrs Nap says.

I'm thinking this could actually turn out to be really GREAT, because Mrs Nap knows I'm a **DUDE 3** fan. I ask her, "Are **DUDE 3** coming to play, then?" and she says, "That would be telling!"

Which probably means NO.

Mum goes back to her seat to watch the rest of the show (even though I'm not playing any more). She says she'll deal with the brush when I get home. (Shame.)

At least I get to watch the other talent-show performances that I didn't see before.

Like Mark Clump and his talking budgie.

Tweet

Say "sausages"

Florence, **AMY** and Indrani singing.

(They're really good!)

Brad Galloway's EXCELLENT dancing.

Some little kids each doing

a line from a poem

(which takes a bit of time).

A few more singers.

And Actors.

And a Ventriloquist.

(My favourite so far.)

When the last performance is over, Mr Keen comes on and all the lights go down.

He says it's been a wonderful show with SO many talented children from Oakfield School. Clap "I'm sure you're all wondering who the **SPECIAL GUESTS** are tonight?"

Clap

Clap

Clap **YESssssssss!**

"Well, we are **VERY** privileged to welcome a **WORLD-FAMOUS** band to our school for a one-off performance – for the very first and possibly the LAST time."

And I'm looking at Derek and Norman, who've come to see who it is as well.

Norman says, Told you **DUDE 3** were coming.

But I can't see them anywhere. Then Mr Keen says, "We need to give a **BIG OAKFIELD SCHOOL WELCOME** to the one and only..."

(Drum rolllllllllllllllllllll ... keep rolllllinggggggggggg...)

"YOU3!"

And for a split second I think Mr Keen has said  DUDE 3 and I'm jumping up and down and cheering when I see ...

Leather trousers

Mr Fullerman, Mr Sprocket and MrsWorthingtash, dressed like they're going to ride motorbikes.

Mrs Worthington has on a FALSE MOUSTACHE (well, I hope it's false).

Me, Norman and Derek look SHOCKED.

Like this...

They start singing...

Get your lesson ready
Head out to the classroom
Get the children running
Practising for SPORTS DAY

We're a NEW teachers' band
Who are born to be MILD
We can keep our cool
In Oakfield School

BORN TO BE MILD.

BORN TO BE MILD.

It's a funny song ... some of the adults are LAUGHING extra hard!

Mr Sprocket and Mr Fullerman are stomping around pretending to be **ROCK** stars. But it's MRS WORTHINGTON who's going CRAZY!

I say to Derek, "This is the MADDEST thing ever!" It might not be DUDE3, but **You3** are so hilarious I almost forget about the brush stuck in my hair.

Then the WHOLE school Clap and Cheer when they finish playing.

CLAP! Hooray CLAP! Hooray

I think the kids in our school will be talking about this teachers' performance
FOR EVER!

Thank you and goodnight

Now the show's over I say bye to everyone and go and meet up with Mum and Dad, who both think the teachers' band was "VERY good!" Dad says, "Makes me want to be in a band!"

Mum gives him a look ⊙̄⊙ and says, "I don't think so."

(I agree with Mum.)

At least Dad has brought the car so I don't have to walk home with this ═══ brush sticking out of my hair. (Which is a relief.)

I can avoid people STARING at me, wondering what I've done. I can't avoid Delia, though. When we get home, Mum and Dad are even telling Delia how FUNNY the teachers' band was.

Delia isn't listening. She's too busy looking at me and shaking her head.

She says,

"How did you do that, idiot?"

So I say, "It was an accident – bit like your **GREEN** hair. Mum's going to help sort it out now."

But before I get the chance to think about what Mum is ACTUALLY going to do (CUT the brush out), she suddenly appears with some scissors

and does this...
SNIP!   SNIP!

Then with a few more **Snip ... Snip ... SnipS...**

It's all finished. I keep my eyes closed until Mum says, "There, all gone now."

I go and take a look in the mirror to see what Mum's done.

And she's right...
It really is all gone now.

Gulp.

Delia catches me looking at my hair. I'm just waiting for her to say something HORRID as usual when she says,

"Don't worry, it will grow back ... eventually."
Which isn't the *worst* thing she could have said, I suppose?

I go upstairs to get ready for bed, then remember to let Derek know the important news – I do a quick doodle and put it up at my window.

NEWS FLASH

THE HAIRBRUSH IS GONE

(and so is some of my hair).

Mum and Dad both come in to say goodnight. They tell me my hair looks very cool shorter. (I'm not so sure.)

 I think it looks a bit odd?

So I'm lying in bed, sort of going to sleep.
But I can't stop thinking about:

1. **YOU3** - so funny!

2. My CHOPPED-off hair.

If I have to sit next to Marcus (when he
stops itching and comes back to school) with
my hair like this, he'll probably just keep
making stupid jokes all the time.

Which will drive me

BONKERS.

Did you cut your hair with a knife and fork?

Hair today gone tomorrow

Then all of a sudden, I get one of MY
VERY BEST-ever ideas that comes to
me in a *FLASH*.

I jump out of bed quickly and grab
a  comb.

Until my hair grows back a bit more, I could just do this?

Let's see if it works...

OH YES!

swap sides!

ANOTHER...

GENIUS IDEA

If I do say so myself...

(Thank you ... thank you.)

How to make a PAPER BANGER

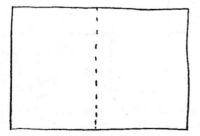

1 A3 paper.

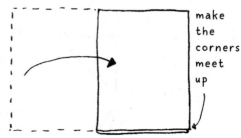

make the corners meet up

2 Fold in half.

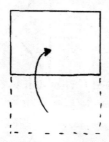

3 Then fold in quarters.

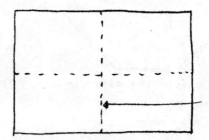

4 Then UNFOLD the paper. There should be nice fold marks now.

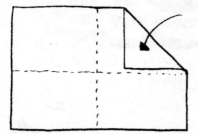

5 Fold down the corner to meet the middle fold line.

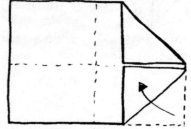

6 Do the same with every corner.

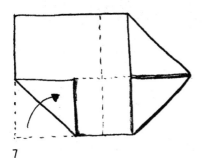

7

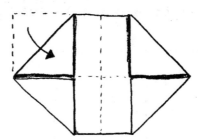

8 Your paper should look like this.

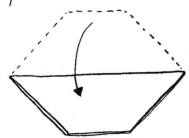

9 Now fold the paper in half, with the flaps inside.

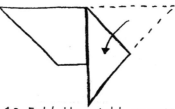

10 Fold the right corner to the middle.

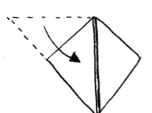

11 Then repeat on the other side.

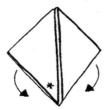

12 Fold the whole banger in half, hold the corners marked, then flick it down HARD.

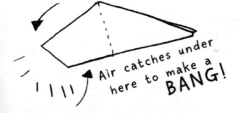

Air catches under here to make a BANG!

BANG!

Q. How do you STOP a GIANT bagel monster

from eating you?

A. Give them the latest Tom Gates book - Tom Gates is ABSOLUTELY FANTASTIC (at Most Things). Out in April 2013

It's just as well that Joey took some other film for our video because the one that Mr Fingle helped set up didn't really work.

For obvious reasons...

This is what our video from Mr Fingle did look like